Rebecca
she ope

She brushed her hands over the soft velvet lining, the scent of cedar and rose potpourri clinging to the inside of the chest. Rebecca then picked up the lacy bride's book. With a wistful sigh she flipped the pages, imagining them filled with signatures of guests.

Guests at her own wedding.

Rebecca then picked up a small children's book. *The Ugly Duckling.* Memories of Grammy's voice reading the story to her night after night echoed in her mind. Hugging the book to her chest, she imagined reading it to her own child one day. Did Grammy foresee a baby in Rebecca's future?

A little boy or girl with dark black hair and green eyes? A little boy who had an amazing similarity to Thomas Emerson?

What in heaven's name was she thinking?

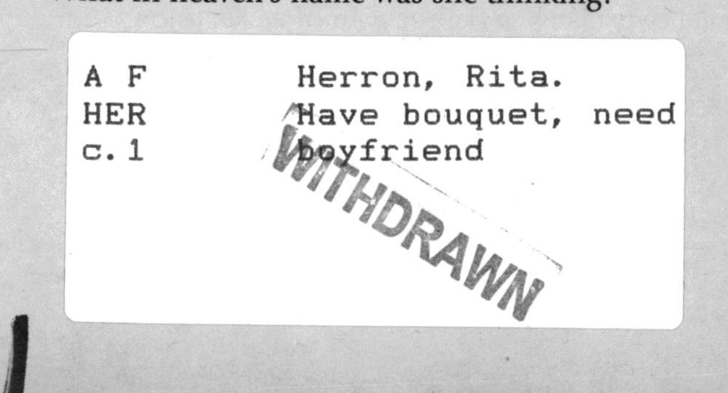

Dear Reader,

What a spectacular lineup of love stories Harlequin American Romance has for you this month as we continue to celebrate our 20th anniversary. Start off with another wonderful title in Cathy Gillen Thacker's DEVERAUX LEGACY series, *Taking Over the Tycoon*. Sexy millionaire Connor Templeton is used to getting whatever—whomever—he wants! But has he finally met his match in one beguiling single mother?

Next, *Fortune's Twins* by Kara Lennox is the latest installment in the MILLIONAIRE, MONTANA continuity series. In this book, a night of passion leaves a "Main Street Millionaire" expecting twins—and has the whole town wondering "Who's the daddy?" After catching a bridal bouquet and opening an heirloom hope chest, a shy virgin dreams about asking her secret crush to father the baby she yearns for, in *Have Bouquet, Need Boyfriend,* part of Rita Herron's HARTWELL HOPE CHESTS series. And don't miss *Inherited: One Baby!* by Laura Marie Altom, in which a handsome bachelor must convince his ex-wife to remarry him in order to keep custody of the adorable orphaned baby left in his care.

Enjoy this month's offerings, and be sure to return each and every month to Harlequin American Romance!

Melissa Jeglinski
Associate Senior Editor
Harlequin American Romance

HAVE BOUQUET, NEED BOYFRIEND

Rita Herron

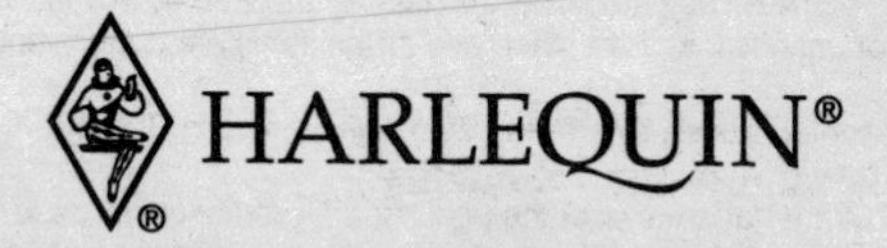

TORONTO • NEW YORK • LONDON
AMSTERDAM • PARIS • SYDNEY • HAMBURG
STOCKHOLM • ATHENS • TOKYO • MILAN • MADRID
PRAGUE • WARSAW • BUDAPEST • AUCKLAND

To all my fans who wrote me wanting more of the Hartwells.
Hope you enjoy!

ISBN 0-373-16975-2

HAVE BOUQUET, NEED BOYFRIEND

This edition published by arrangement with Harlequin Books S.A.

Visit us at www.eHarlequin.com

Printed in U.S.A.

ABOUT THE AUTHOR

Award-winning author Rita Herron wrote her first book when she was twelve, but didn't think real people grew up to be writers. Now she writes so she doesn't have to get a *real* job. A former kindergarten teacher and workshop leader, she traded her storytelling for kids for romance and writes romantic comedies and romance suspense. She lives in Georgia with her own romance hero and three kids. She loves to hear from readers so please write her at P.O. Box 921225, Norcross, GA 30092-1225 or visit her Web site at www.ritaherron.com.

Books by Rita Herron

HARLEQUIN AMERICAN ROMANCE

820—HIS-AND-HERS TWINS
859—HAVE GOWN, NEED GROOM*
872—HAVE BABY, NEED BEAU*
883—HAVE HUSBAND, NEED HONEYMOON*
944—THE RANCHER WORE SUITS
975—HAVE BOUQUET, NEED BOYFRIEND*

* The Hartwell Hope Chests

HARLEQUIN INTRIGUE

486—SEND ME A HERO
523—HER EYEWITNESS
556—FORGOTTEN LULLABY
601—SAVING HIS SON
660—SILENT SURRENDER†
689—MEMORIES OF MEGAN†
710—THE CRADLE MISSION†

† Nighthawk Island

My dearest Rebecca,

You are a very special granddaughter because you remind me so much of myself when I was your age. You were the first of Bert's daughters, the one who brought a deep love into his marriage that cemented the bond between him and your mother.

But you were the one who suffered the most when your mother died. Although your own heart was aching, you pushed your feelings aside to comfort your father and your little sister in their sorrow.

You showed such strength that the rest of us gained courage from you. But when you retreated to that silent place where you grieved, you never quite came back.

Always steady and strong, dependable and caring, you are loyal and trusting to a fault. Believe in yourself now, Rebecca. Take time to nurture your own dreams and talents, and love yourself the way you love others.

I wish for you happiness, true love and a man who will give you all the joy a partner can.

Love you always,
Grammy Rose

Chapter One

"Who's getting married next?" Alison Hartwell Broussard waved her bridal bouquet of roses in the air in open invitation, looking pointedly at her cousin Rebecca.

A few shrieks answered in reply. "Me!"

"No, me!"

A quiver of longing rippled through Rebecca, but she remained silent, hugging her arms around herself in a protective embrace as she stood beneath the sprawling branches of a live oak. She was the *least* likely of all the single and female bridesmaids at her cousin Alison's wedding to tie the knot.

Her model-gorgeous sister, Suzanne, would probably be next. That is, if she ever decided to settle down with one man. Right now, *marriage* and *monogamy* were two words missing from Suzanne's vocabulary.

Rebecca was the very opposite.

She ached for marriage. For one man to love her and hold her and make her feel special. To give her a child.

Unfortunately, the man she yearned for happened to

be Thomas Emerson, a man who had once been engaged to Alison.

A man who had his pick of women in town. A man who might still be in love with Alison. A man who'd barely noticed Rebecca.

Well, except for the time she'd dropped an entire platter of pastries on his head at Vivi Broussard's wedding. He had gazed at her through the whipped cream dripping from his hair as if she might possibly be the biggest klutz in the world. Which she was.

Especially when she got nervous. And being around Thomas Emerson made her *extremely* nervous.

"Come on, ladies, line up." Alison stepped beneath the trellis of roses, an early-winter breeze carrying the spicy scent of flowers through the air. "Brady and I are ready to leave. He's finally promised me a honeymoon." She slid her arm around Brady's waist. "I only had to marry him twice to get it."

Laughter and cheers erupted. Alison's sisters' husbands, Jake Tippins and Seth Broadhurst, grinned wickedly, obviously remembering highlights of their own honeymoons.

Brady slung an arm around his new wife. "Honey, it'll be worth the wait."

More laughter followed, envy mushrooming inside Rebecca. Her three cousins had all married this past year in the gazebo on top of Pine Mountain at Grammy Rose's, and their husbands obviously doted on them. She wanted that kind of love, that mind-altering, earth-shattering bond with a man.

But every time she got physically close to a man, she lost her cool. Rational conversation fled, and she stumbled all over her size-seven feet. And sometimes, God help her, sometimes she even stuttered.

"Becca, come on." Suzanne jerked her toward the small crowd of women gathering on the lawn, their long dresses fluttering in the wind. "Angie and Caitlin are about to attack Alison for those flowers."

Rebecca laughed at her twenty-three-year-old twin cousins—daughters of her aunt Shelby who giggled and squealed—vying for the place in front of Alison. Although the twins shared a sibling rivalry born of being identical, they also shared a loving sisterhood, as did Hannah, Mimi and Alison. For some reason, she and Suzanne had never quite had that connection.

Probably because they were so different.

Another stab of envy assaulted Rebecca as Mimi nestled her three-month old baby to her chest. Rebecca's own biological clock beat inside her like a drum. She desperately wanted a baby.

But a husband had to come first.

"Back to earth, Becca." Suzanne waved her hand in front of Rebecca's eyes, but Thomas gazed their way, and Rebecca froze. A frown marred his lips, his charcoal-black hair gleaming in the early evening light. The immediate pull of attraction that engulfed her slid through her nerve endings, sending a frenzy of delicious sensations spiraling through her. Sensations that paralyzed her.

His six-foot-plus muscular frame filled out his dark suit. His broad shoulders almost seemed massive in the crisp white dress shirt. The sparkle of laughter normally present in his light-green eyes was replaced by a dark, faraway look, arousing her curiosity. Was he wishing Alison had married him instead of Brady?

Contemplating going to him and offering a comforting hand, Rebecca started across the lawn. But her heel caught on a twig. She took a step forward and nearly plunged to the ground. Yelping, she reached for something to steady her, or at least break her fall, but found nothing to hold on to, not a chair or a tree or a table in sight. Thomas pitched forward as if to break her fall, although he wasn't near enough to reach her, but Suzanne, ever the graceful one, slid a long manicured hand beneath her elbow, catching Rebecca first. Mortification stung Rebecca's cheeks.

A fraction of a second later, Thomas raised his gaze, the dark intensity disappearing as a slow smile spread across his face.

Rebecca's heart fluttered.

Suzanne poked her. "Wow, who is that hottie eating the groom's cake?"

Her heart sank.

If Suzanne wanted him, even though she lived miles away in Atlanta, she would have him. Suzanne *always* got what she wanted.

"Thom-Thomas Em-erson, the OB-GYN—" She took a deep breath to steady her voice. "He works with Hannah."

Suzanne whistled beneath her breath. "Whew, a girl might be tempted to tear up her little black book for him."

Rebecca gulped. Thomas continued to stare, his gaze almost unnerving this time.

He had to be looking at Suzanne. Everyone stared at her dark-haired, incredibly exotic-looking sibling. Not that she could blame them. Suzanne was beautiful. Dazzling. Mesmerizing. And, darn it, she was even nice, so Rebecca couldn't hate her. Suzanne didn't try to get all the attention. People were just drawn to her.

But Rebecca was the mousy blonde who hid behind books and art and wire-rimmed glasses. The impossibly shy one who couldn't talk or walk without tripping over her own tongue or feet.

"Let's hurry, she's getting ready to throw the roses!" Suzanne gently pushed Rebecca forward just as Alison released the flowers. The bouquet soared through the air, bouncing first from Caitlin's hands to Angie's, then finally landing with a thump on Rebecca's head. She reached for the arrangement, but the ribbon caught on the stem of her glasses, dangling over her eyes, blinding her, and a thorn from the rose stabbed her finger.

THOMAS EMERSON FOUGHT a laugh as he watched Rebecca Hartwell struggle with the bridal bouquet. She was such a sweet, fragile-looking woman that his battered heart lurched every time he saw her.

But he refused to get involved with another woman right now. Even kind-hearted blondes with big blue eyes and curves that might be sinful. That is, if she didn't hide them beneath those baggy dresses.

He pulled at his collar, a bead of sweat trickling down his neck. This rash of weddings lately had definitely affected him, probably the reason he'd proposed to Alison a few months ago. But in retrospect he realized he wasn't ready for marriage.

Instead he intended to focus on his career. Although he currently shared a practice with Hannah Hartwell, he had bigger goals. The very reason he'd been watching Rebecca in the first place. Not because he was attracted to the shy little nymph.

No, he wanted to meet Bert Hartwell, her father. Dr. Hartwell was a renowned plastic surgeon and chairman of the board of the new women's medical facility in Atlanta. The hospital boasted the latest in technology, research and cutting-edge medical techniques that Thomas wanted to be a part of. He had hoped to see Dr. Hartwell with Rebecca, but apparently he hadn't shown up at his niece's wedding.

Rumor had it he was off on a honeymoon of his own, his fourth, to be exact.

Odd. His daughters hadn't attended his wedding.

And he'd also heard that Bert didn't exactly get along with Alison's father, Wiley. Apparently they'd had some kind of rift way back when.

Hmm, an interesting family. Not that he could be critical; his own family had disintegrated years ago.

A moment of concern tugged at him as he noticed how forlorn Rebecca seemed in the midst of the giggling women as she tried to untangle the ribbon from her glasses, but he brushed it aside.

Nice guys finished last.

He had learned that lesson well.

First, he'd lost the job he'd really wanted after med school to a guy who claimed to have been his friend. Then he'd lost Alison.

Hell, he'd really never had her.

His pride smarted, but he reminded himself Alison was happy and that was all that mattered. He certainly wouldn't have tried to hold on to someone who didn't love him.

Was there something about him that was unlovable?

He contemplated the way his mother had acted after she'd lost his baby brother, the way his father had so easily deserted him when his mother had thrown him out. Of course, his dad had been hurting as well, especially when his mom had admitted that she'd only used him to have another baby… Still, why hadn't he been enough for them?

Maybe he'd been looking for a way to settle down in this quaint town and he'd hoped Alison was that key. But he *didn't* really want to stay in Sugar Hill the rest of his life, did he?

He had other goals in mind. To land that job at the new women's center. Thomas had an interview scheduled in a few weeks. Getting to know Bert on a personal level would give him the inside scoop on Hartwell's theories and goals, and the interview would go smoother.

Perhaps Rebecca would introduce him to her father. He'd overheard Mimi and Hannah discussing plans for a surprise birthday party for their grandmother. Wiley and Bert would both attend. If he could swing an invitation, it would be the perfect opportunity to meet Bert. He'd considered asking Hannah to introduce him, but he wasn't ready to tell her he intended to leave the practice yet. If he asked Rebecca, he could keep his intentions quiet for a while. No sense stirring up trouble at work unless he had the new job in the bag.

A red blush stained Rebecca's cheeks as she plucked the bouquet from her head. Hopefully, she wouldn't run from him the way she had at Brady's sister's Vivi's wedding when she'd dropped those cream puffs on his head.

She'd acted as if he was the big bad wolf ready to gobble her up.

Though he wasn't the big bad wolf, he was through being Mr. Nice Guy. From now on, he would pursue his goals with a vengeance. And landing that job topped his list.

He would do whatever was necessary in order to secure it.

Rebecca and her grandmother ambled up the wrap-around porch, heads bowed, voices hushed. Thomas hunched his shoulders against the chilly December air and strode across the lawn to catch Rebecca before she left. Then he would set his plan in motion.

REBECCA SLIPPED INTO her Grammy Rose's parlor, breathing in the essence of her grandmother in the polished antiques and silver-framed photos of family and friends. She had always loved this room, loved the needlepoint pillows and china cups, the smell of Grammy's rose-scented sachets filling the air, the scrapbooks full of treasured gifts from each of her grandchildren.

Someday she wanted a room like this in her own home. Just like she wanted a house full of kids, and then grandchildren. She would keep rose-scented potpourri in the house and homemade doilies on the coffee table, and keep pictures of all her children and grandchildren framed on the wall.

"It's time you take your hope chest home," Grammy said.

Rebecca's throat tightened at the sight of the ornately carved wooden chest. Alison and her sisters had talked as if their hope chests carried some kind of secret power. Like an omen for the future. Or maybe Grammy Rose did.

Did the hope chest mean a wedding might be in the future for her?

No, Rebecca couldn't allow herself to believe in such fantasies.

"But, Grammy, I'm not getting married."

"Nonsense. Of course you are."

Rebecca stared wide-eyed at the chest. She itched to reach out and touch it, to open it and discover what treasures lay inside.

But she couldn't admit those feelings aloud.

"No, I...I don't want to get married," she forced herself to say. "I...I like my life just the way it is."

THOMAS OVERHEARD Rebecca talking to her grandmother and breathed a sigh of relief. Rebecca didn't want marriage, so he didn't have to worry about her getting the wrong idea if he cozied up to her.

Thank goodness.

He didn't want to hurt her. But being friendly with her might help his chances of getting the new job. Then he could move on with his life and make a name for himself in the medical world. And he'd finally fulfill that promise he'd made to himself years ago.

Yes, Rebecca would be the key to him leaving Sugar Hill.

The voices behind the door grew hushed, and he strained to hear, then stepped back, ashamed at himself for eavesdropping. Suddenly the door swung open, and Grammy Rose's pointed chin jutted up in surprise, her eyes sparkling.

"Hey there, young man." She threaded a strand of

gray hair back inside the pearl clip at her nape. "Dr. Emerson, isn't it?"

Heat warmed Thomas's neck. She didn't know he'd been listening, did she? "Yes, ma'am."

"Listen, son, could you do me a favor?"

"I'll do what I can." Surely, she wasn't inventing an illness for him to treat, like a few of the women patients who swarmed his office. He'd never seen anything like life in Sugar Hill.

"Good. My granddaughter Rebecca needs help carrying her hope chest to the car." She gestured toward the room behind her. "She's right there in the parlor."

Thomas frowned. Didn't women receive hope chests when they were engaged? *Odd.* He'd just heard Rebecca say she wasn't interested in marriage.

REBECCA SLID A FINGER around the lock of the chest and released it, her heart pounding when the top sprang open. She *should* wait until she arrived home to look inside the hope chest. But curiosity replaced common sense, and she lifted the lid.

Dark-red velvet lined the chest and a piece of antique lace was folded over the top of the contents. Her fingers traced the fabrics, reveling in the richness of texture as she slowly moved the lace aside. A white bride's book lay nestled there, its top embossed with silver wedding bells.

Footsteps suddenly sounded against the hardwood floor, the loose board at the parlor door squeaking. She slammed the lid closed, then swung around to find Thomas Emerson standing in the doorway.

"Your grandmother asked me to help you take something to the car."

His deep voice spun a dizzying web around her senses. She opened her mouth to speak but barely managed to sputter a no.

He inched inside the room anyway, his masculine presence nearly overpowering the room.

"Thanks, but I...I can get it." Rebecca fidgeted atop the small wooden stool, wishing she could shrink the hope chest and keep it out of sight. He might think she was hinting at something.

Like the fact that she wanted a husband and family of her own.

His green eyes radiated warmth as he gazed down at her. No wonder all the ladies in town threw themselves at him. "Come on, Rebecca. I don't mind." He moved around her, planting his big hands on his hips as he studied the box. "Will it fit in your car?"

She nodded, her palms sweaty as she stood. Oh, heck. She couldn't very well deny him or she'd look like an idiot. "In...the back."

He lifted the chest in one fluid motion, then gestured toward the doorway. Rebecca grabbed her purse and trotted forward, willing herself not to fall on her face or break her neck before she reached the car.

On the porch she hugged her grandmother and said a hasty goodbye, faintly aware most of the other guests had left. Hannah and Mimi were huddled inside the cluster of their father and mother. Her heart squeezed with envy. Sometimes she felt closer to her uncle Wiley than her own father. She searched for her sister to say goodbye, but Suzanne had apparently left to hit some of the after-Christmas sales with the twins.

Seconds later she managed to find her trusted clunker station wagon at the foot of the long, winding drive, where she'd parked between two trees. Thomas's silver Porsche convertible was parked across the drive, her father's Suburban several yards away by some pines. She watched as Thomas slid the hope chest into the back, her breath catching at the sight of his dark hair falling over his eyes.

"There you go." He raked the lock of hair back in a gesture so manly that she had to swallow.

"Thanks." She wanted to say more but her tongue caught on her teeth.

A smile curved his mouth, the wind tousling the lock of hair into disarray again, making him even more sexy. "Are you in a hurry? We could grab some coffee and talk."

Talk?

No, talk was impossible. Her tongue was *superglued* to her teeth now.

She shook her head. "I...have—" she paused and cleared her throat "—have to hurry home."

He jammed his hands in his pockets and studied her as she darted past him and into the car. "Are you sure? Rebecca..."

She ignored the fact that he followed her to the driver's side and waved him off. "Thanks again." Rebecca's hands shook as she shoved the keys into the ignition, her mind tumbling with questions. Had Thomas really asked her out?

And if so, why?

It didn't matter. She was a flirting failure and a disaster at the sex talk most women seemed so comfortable with these days. A real dinosaur at relationships.

She pressed the clutch, turned the key and sighed

as the engine roared to life. Putting it into reverse, she rolled backward. Then she glanced in her rearview window and saw Thomas jump aside.

Dear God, she'd almost hit him.

He threw up a hand and waved anyway, and she panicked and pressed the gas again. But she'd forgotten to shift into drive and the car shot backward again. Gravel spun out sideways, the ground flew by under her, then her car lurched to a stop, metal crunching and glass shattering. Her neck jerked back, then sideways, then snapped forward. Her forehead and chest slammed against the steering wheel. The horn blared. She squeezed the steering wheel with white-knuckled hands. Breathing in slowly, she lifted her head and looked over her shoulder to survey the damage. Her heart clamored to a stop. The top of the hope chest had fallen over, the contents spilling out. She peeked beyond, cringing.

She had just smashed into Thomas's brand-new convertible. It looked like a broken pretzel.

Chapter Two

The sound of metal crunching and glass breaking rang in Thomas's ears as he ran toward Rebecca's car. But his heart pounded with worry. What if Rebecca was hurt?

He wrenched open the door, his pulse hammering at the sight of her trembling body. Her head was thrown forward, her hands clenching the steering wheel, her face shadowed by strands of hair that had fallen forward. Worse, her body was so still it seemed lifeless.

Had she hit her head?

"Rebecca?" He hesitated, knowing he couldn't move her; she might be seriously injured. But he had to know if she was conscious. He pressed two fingers to her neck to feel for a pulse. She trembled beneath his touch, a shiver rippling through her.

A low cry tore from her throat as she turned tear-stained eyes to him. "I'm so-o-o sorry."

Relief surged through him. A red lump protruded on her forehead, and her glasses hung askew, but, thank God, she was okay.

"Are you hurt?" He waited, his heart pounding when she simply stared at him with glazed eyes.

"Rebecca, please answer me. Where are you hurt?" He quickly surveyed her with his eyes to check for blood or protruding bones, but didn't spot any major injuries. She hadn't been wearing her seat belt though. Not a good sign. "Rebecca—"

"I'm such an idiot."

He eased her back to rest against the seat, gently removed her glasses, then, with a finger below her eyes, checked her pupils. "Did you hit your head hard?"

She shook her head, her wide-eyed gaze full of shock.

"You weren't wearing your seat belt?"

She glanced down in a daze. "Was…going to."

"Your ribs? Did you hit the steering wheel?"

She nodded dumbly, her expression lost. "I…your car."

"Forget about the damn car, just tell me if you're hurting somewhere." He reached for the front of her billowy bridesmaid dress to check for injuries to her chest, but she pushed his hands away in horror. "Rebecca, I'm just trying to examine you."

"I'm fine." She sniffled, her body shaking. "But I ruined your…your Porsche. I meant to go forward, but I forgot to shift gears and then the car shot back so fast—"

"I said to forget the car. Now if you won't let me check you here, I'll call an ambulance."

"No." She grabbed his hands and clung to him. "I'm okay, but I feel so stupid…" A wail escaped her, long and quavery.

His heart squeezed at the misery in her voice, so he cupped her face in his hands. ''Stop worrying. I have insurance.''

That luscious lower lip of hers trembled again, the color draining from her face. He couldn't stand it, he pulled her against the crook of his neck and rocked her, murmuring soft words of comfort. She felt fragile and small and more womanly than he'd expected. Protective instincts kicked in, warring with a sudden realization that her minty breath was tickling his neck, and the subtle scent of her feminine perfume was awakening sensations better left dormant.

''What was that noise?'' Shouts erupted behind them and he could hear footsteps beating a path down the graveled drive. He pulled away, standing by the car and turning to face Rebecca's relatives. Hannah, Jake, and Wiley Hartwell jogged down the path, Wiley heaving as he pushed his way to the front.

''Everyone okay?'' Wiley yelled.

''I think so.'' Thomas frowned at Wiley's taxed breathing. The last thing he needed was the man to have a heart attack and send Rebecca into full shock.

''Rebecca, baby, are you all right?'' Wiley leaned his hands on his pudgy knees, peering into the car. Jake and Hannah approached, Mimi, Seth, and Grammy Rose behind them, their faces full of concern.

''Mercy me,'' Grammy Rose murmured.

''Becca, are you all right?'' Hannah and Mimi both asked at once.

''Yes.'' Rebecca wiped her eyes with the back of her hand, slipped her wire-rimmed spectacles back on her nose and grabbed the door to pull herself out. Thomas slid a hand in to help her. She was still shaking but managed to get out of the car, not meeting his gaze.

He silently surveyed her again and was thankful not to see any blood.

"But I ruined Thomas's car."

The entire family pivoted, each gaping at the mangled metal with various stunned looks. She had collided with the driver's side, smashing the front door like a piece of cardboard. The windshield and windows had imploded with the impact, and glass pellets covered the beige leather. Her own station wagon had suffered as well. The bumper was warped, the tailpipe bent at an odd angle. But the clunker had already seen its better days; the faded green paint was chipped and peeling off in strips.

"It is kind of dented," Mimi said in a low voice.

"The passenger side is still intact," Hannah added cheerfully.

As if to mock her, the hub cap from the right-front tire fell off, rolled toward her and settled into a spin at her feet.

"Mercy me," Grammy Rose whispered.

"You can still open the door," Jake offered, obviously trying to be optimistic.

But when he yanked on the door handle to prove his point, the wretched metal came off in his hands with a crunch. The left tire let out a whooshing sound, then popped and the tire deflated right in front of their eyes.

Rebecca's sob caught in horror.

"But you're all right?" Hannah inched forward as if to emphasize that Rebecca's safety was more important than the automobile.

Mortification stung her face as she pointed to the broken piece of metal. ''I can't believe I did all that.''

''Shh, now, don't fret.'' Grammy Rose patted Rebecca's back. ''We all have accidents, sweetie. I'll never forget the time I ran my car into the front porch. Broke up a hornets' nest. Those dad-gummed bees attacked me, almost bit me in the behind.''

''Yeah, I've had some fender-benders myself,'' Mimi chimed in. ''Even worse than this. Right in our own driveway.''

''I can vouch for that,'' Seth added.

Mimi poked him with her elbow. ''It wasn't my fault that garbage can jumped in the way. Or that you parked the minivan so close to my Miata.''

Seth opened his mouth to argue, but Mimi's mutinous glare stopped him. Thomas almost laughed at Jake and Wiley's skeptical expressions. Apparently Rebecca and Mimi had a reputation for freak crashes.

''Well, it's just metal,'' Grammy Rose said, smacking her lips.

''Pricy metal.'' Jake whistled, propping the door against the side of the car.

This time Hannah's glare cut across the crowd. ''Fixable metal,'' Hannah added. ''All it needs is a good body shop mechanic.''

''Or a miracle worker,'' Rebecca muttered between sobs.

''Nah, baby, it's fixable.'' Wiley hugged her to his side. ''It's just not drivable now.''

''He's right.'' Thomas's gaze flickered to the customized paint chipping off from the collision.

Mimi bounced the baby on her shoulder. ''You want Seth to call a tow truck?''

Thomas nodded. "Thanks. I'd appreciate that."

"Nonsense." Wiley waved a beefy hand. "I'll phone my service to tow it. You can borrow a car from my used-car lot till yours is fixed. Now, pull yourself together, Bec, darlin'."

Rebecca sniffed as she accepted her uncle's handkerchief and swiped at her nose.

"That would be great, Mr. Hartwell." Thomas cast another look at Rebecca, grateful she'd stopped crying. What had she expected him to do? Turn into a tyrant because she'd totaled his car?

REBECCA DABBED AT HER EYES with her uncle's hankie. How could she have done such a stupid thing?

And how could Thomas stand there so calmly when she had destroyed what must have been his dream car, a Porsche that cost more money than she earned in *two* years. Men usually obsessed about their automobiles. They worshipped them more than their women, more than the remote control.

Worse, now her insurance would skyrocket, she'd probably have to take a second job to pay her bills, and everyone in town would talk about her klutzy ways, just as they had in high school years ago.

Thunder rumbled above, the darkening sky hinting at a winter storm. Rain began to drizzle and chaos erupted, everyone suddenly racing for the house.

Grammy Rose hugged her one more time. "Don't fret, everything will work out all right. At least the hope chest wasn't damaged."

Rebecca bit the inside of her cheek. Great. She had a hope chest but no man. And the only man she'd wanted since her dating disasters in high school was standing beside her, his car crunched like a tin can because she lost control of her senses every time he was near.

For all she knew, the crash could have broken some of the things in her chest, too. She was too afraid to look.

Lightning streaked through the cluster of pine trees, another clap of thunder booming closer. ''I'll make sure the tow truck picks up the car,'' Wiley offered. ''Bec, you wanna give the doc a ride back to town?''

Rebecca's face blanched.

''Good idea,'' Thomas said with a grin. ''You don't mind taking me home, do you?''

Rebecca gaped at him in surprise. She couldn't very well turn him down when she was responsible for his dilemma.

''I...sure.''

Thomas pointed inside the station wagon. ''It looks like some of your stuff spilled out. We'd better put it back before we go.''

The bride's book lay on the floor, a blue garter belt beside it.

''No, it's all right.'' She pushed Thomas toward the car. ''Let's go before the storm gets any worse.''

And I do anything else stupid. Rebecca ran to the other side and jumped in. Thomas took the passenger seat, buckled his seat belt, then stretched his left arm along the back of the seat, calm as a cucumber.

Darn him.

Rebecca glanced at her clenched hands, then slowly met his gaze. ''I'm surprised you'd want to ride with me. Aren't you afraid I'll kill you on the way home?''

THOMAS CHUCKLED. Hell, yeah he was, but he couldn't admit it without seeming like a coward. ''No, of course not.'' He shifted, but the broken springs from the tattered seat protested, then jabbed him in the behind. Rebecca glanced his way and nearly ran off the road.

The deep dropoff on his side swam before his eyes. ''Rebecca!''

She snapped her eyes back to the highway, her mouth dropping open as she jerked the wheel to the left.

''Are you sure you're all right? I could drive if you're feeling dizzy from the accident.''

She pursed her lips. ''No, I'm f-fine.''

Rain splattered the windshield, and the car windows fogged up, cocooning the two of them inside the vehicle. He wondered if Rebecca had bought this jalopy from her uncle; if so, he hoped Wiley had cut her a good deal. It wasn't worth a dime.

Was she was always this nervous around men or did her reaction have something to do with him? He'd seen her conversing with customers in the bookstore. She handled herself with grace, her knowledge about the book market extraordinary. And she laughed and joked with her cousins as if she were perfectly at ease.

Maybe she just didn't find him attractive. The thought smarted. Especially since most of the women in town seemed to like him.

''Rebecca, can I ask you something?''

She winced and slowed the car as if driving and talking weren't compatible activities. ''If it's about the insurance, I d-do have it. You can get my card from my purse.''

"It's not about the insurance." He sighed. "I wish you'd relax and forget about it. I'm not worried."

"But how can I forget?" She glanced at her tiny silver purse, which lay on the seat, the contents spilled, a tampon poking out of the top, then jerked her attention back to the road, the oncoming lights of a truck glaringly bright. "That car costs a fortune. And I destroyed it in less than a minute."

"Money isn't the most important thing in the world," he said with conviction. Although he was frugal with his money. With good reason. After all, he'd grown up in a fairly low-income family where money was sparse and love even more so. But he couldn't bring himself to be mad at Rebecca when she was so upset herself.

A nervous flutter of her eyes followed. "I didn't mean it like that, Thomas. I'm not implying that you're materialistic...." She let the sentence trail off, obviously shaken by the turn of the conversation.

"I didn't mean to imply you thought I was—"

"I didn't think you were."

His head was spinning. "Well, thanks for that. I was beginning to think you didn't like me."

"What?" The shock in her voice surprised him.

"You run every time I get near you." He pried his fingers off the door handle, forcing his hand to relax on his thigh. "I thought maybe you'd heard some bad things about me or something."

"Bad things?" Her gaze found him again, her blue eyes luminous in the foggy interior. "No, I've only heard good things about you. What bad things would I hear?"

"None." At least not that he knew of.

His gaze fell to her scalloped neckline, which revealed a hint of creamy skin and rounded breasts. "I've heard nice things about you, too."

She hit a pothole, and the car jerked sideways. An oncoming car blasted its horn. He grabbed the dash, and she swung the car back in line just in time to avoid a head-on collision. "I...good."

"Well, now we've got that settled," he said, finding the radio. "We can relax."

Like hell. Maybe some soft music would calm her. He certainly needed something to steady his nerves, considering the way she kept courting the embankment. And that sultry scent enveloping her was rattling other nerves that had no business being awakened.

He simply wanted a friendship with Rebecca Hartwell. An uncomplicated, platonic friendship with no feelings or commitments or expectations to hinder him from his goal of leaving Sugar Hill.

"So, why did you go into medicine?"

His fingers tightened on the knob. "I like the challenge. And no matter how many babies I deliver, the miracle of birth never ceases to astound me."

"Babies are wonderful." Rebecca's voice softened. "I love watching Mimi with Maggie Rose. That little girl is adorable."

"Both her parents dote on her."

Rebecca laughed. "I'm glad it worked out for them to be together. I thought Mimi might raise the baby alone for a while."

Thomas nodded. He'd heard something about that. Once again his thoughts turned to his own mother and how difficult his teenage years had been. "Being a single mom is tough. I admire women who raise children alone these days."

"Yeah, I miss my mom. She died when I was young," Rebecca admitted.

Thomas placed a hand on her shoulder. "I'm sorry, Rebecca. I lost my mom a while back, but she was alive when I was little."

A few moments of companionable silence stretched taut between them. Then she hit another bump and her purse flew from the seat to the floor. The tampon rolled out. She blushed, then reached for it.

He grimaced. Good grief, he was an OB-GYN.

The car swerved sideways, and he yanked up the purse, stuffed the tampon inside and closed it for her. Her lips snapped shut.

Then she hit another bump in the road, and the chest in the back bounced up and slammed down with a thump. He angled his head to see it. "What's in that box, anyway?"

Rebecca's gaze darted everywhere but at him. "Just some junk for a garage sale."

He lapsed into silence as he remembered the dozens of garage sales his mother had had. She'd sold everything she could stand to part with just to provide for them. He'd hated seeing their things being hocked to strangers for mere pocket change.

Surely Rebecca wasn't that desperate for money.

If she was, she'd have a hell of a time paying her insurance if the company raised it after they covered the damages to his car.

But her finances were not his problem, he reminded himself, battling a twinge of sympathy. He was not playing Mr. Nice Guy again. He would befriend Rebecca so she could introduce him to her father, then he'd secure the job and move to Atlanta.

Nothing more.

A HALF HOUR LATER Rebecca's insides still quivered. What had happened to her today? Not only had she ruined Thomas's Porsche, but she'd damn near run off the road and *killed* him. Then she'd lied to him about the silly hope chest.

But she didn't want him to think she was husband hunting, that she would mistake his kindness for an advance. Because Thomas Emerson was the nicest man she'd ever met. And the sexiest. And someone was going to be the luckiest woman alive one day to have him for a husband.

Of course, that someone would not be her.

Memories of at least three painful past relationships traipsed through her mind, trampling her mood altogether. Memories of men who had used her to get to Suzanne.

No, Thomas wasn't like those men. He was trustworthy and sincere and helped women through his work. He would never use a woman. Although, she had overheard him asking Hannah about Suzanne when she'd gone for punch.

She veered onto the interstate toward his house, grateful for the soft jazz music filling the tense silence. Once she dropped him at his house, she wouldn't have to face him again. She could handle the insurance information over the phone and never have to look into those startling green eyes again. As long as she didn't see him, she could put him firmly out of her mind.

Then she wouldn't have to drool over him and want the man so badly.

After all, she was a realist. She refused to torture herself and dream about things she could never have.

Like Thomas Emerson.

Chapter Three

Thomas shook his head as Rebecca drove away. She was an enigma. He'd finally grown tired of the strained silence in the car and had ventured into asking her about a book he'd ordered that hadn't yet arrived.

She had transformed into an intelligent, well-spoken woman.

The past half hour they'd enjoyed a long discussion of various popular titles as well as nonfiction topics. Rebecca was well-read and insightful, and had even argued with him about the authors of some hard-to-find classics. But when he'd suggested they stop by her place so he could help her unload that chest full of garage sale items, she'd grown flustered again. She'd claimed her neighbor, Jerry Ruthers, would assist her instead.

Was this guy Jerry her boyfriend? Was he the reason she'd rushed to get home and had refused Thomas's offer of coffee?

An odd feeling pinched his gut. Maybe it was from the chocolate groom's cake he'd eaten at Alison's wedding. No, probably from the jostling his body had been subjected to on the harrowing ride home.

He walked inside his house, smiling at the expanse of polished hardwood and detailed molding. As a child, he'd never imagined owning a house like this, one with space and class. He tossed his keys onto the marble table in the foyer and stopped in the den, his gaze riveted to the Palladian glass window overlooking his backyard. A cluster of oaks so ancient the branches swayed with age provided shade while a fish pond added more visual interest.

Pride swelled in his chest at his accomplishments.

Still, material things weren't enough. His thirst for knowledge couldn't be quenched. He'd vowed to learn everything he could about high-risk deliveries. A child's life might depend on his skill and expertise.

The key to reaching his goals lay in that job in Atlanta.

Now he just had to devise a plan to see Rebecca again and swing an invitation to her grandmother's surprise birthday party so he could meet Bert Hartwell.

REBECCA HURRIEDLY PLACED the bride's book and a book on dream analysis back into the chest and shut it, not wanting any of her neighbors to see the contents of her hope chest. Ignoring the growing chill in the air, she tugged and pulled at the hope chest, trying desperately to remove it from the back of the station wagon, but the bumps she'd taken had wedged the corner of the chest into the side by the spare tire, and it was completely stuck. The effort made her already sore chest ache even more. She felt a sharp pain in it each time she took a deep breath, too. She must have bruised her ribs. They couldn't be broken or she would be in much worse pain. Right?

She shoved again, and mashed her finger. Why hadn't she had the courage to accept Thomas's offer of help?

She couldn't ask him to assist her when she'd already inconvenienced him. No telling how long it would take to repair his car. Granted he could borrow something from Uncle Wiley's lot to drive in the interim, but she had no idea what kind of vehicle he'd get for a loaner.

Uncle Wiley did not have any brand-new silver Porches on his used-car lot.

"Yo, Becky." Jerry Ruthers, Rebecca's neighbor who'd dogged her for a date ever since she'd moved into the small duplex next to his, loped toward her, pulling baggy jeans up beneath his sagging belly. "Need a hand?" He flexed his muscles, the bulge shoving the short sleeve of his white T-shirt up, revealing arms layered in thick, dark hair and a cigarette pack.

Rebecca cringed. "Thanks, but I can—"

He pushed her aside, yanked out the hope chest much the same as Thomas had done, except Jerry added a melodramatic grunt, and sweat poured down his unshaven face. He thundered toward the front door, his jeans slipping down his backside.

She hurried after him, deciding to buy him a belt to hold up his pants in exchange for his good deed.

"Where do you want it, Becky?"

She hated being called Becky, but she unlocked the door and ignored the nickname, not wanting to prolong their conversation. "The den is fine." She gestured toward the blue ruffled sofa and watched him heave as he lowered the chest to the faded beige carpet.

He whistled, wiped at his forehead with his arm, then grinned. ''What you got in there, sugar cakes?''

''Some things from my grandmother.'' She inched back toward the door, hoping he would follow. She didn't intend to discuss the hope chest with him any more than she had with Thomas.

''Dang it, you look pretty today.'' His gaze traveled over her dark green bridesmaid's dress, lingering at her cleavage before dropping in appreciation to her silver spiked heels. ''Where you been? You look like a Christmas tree, all lit up and sparkling.''

''My cousin's wedding.'' Rebecca ignored his come-hither grin. ''She got married at my grandmother's house.'' Jerry was the only man who'd shown an interest in her recently, Rebecca thought morosely. She should try to see him in a romantic light. After all, she *never* stuttered or had klutzy attacks when he was around, but she couldn't muster up an ounce of attraction toward him. She yawned, her chest pinching again, and hoped he'd take the hint.

He didn't. He stood with one leg cocked sideways as if waiting on an invitation to stay. ''Wanna get some dinner? They got chili burgers on the special at Pokey Slims tonight.''

Pokey Slims was a biker bar on the other side of town. Lots of beer drinking, tattooed men and cigarette smoke. ''No, thanks. I'm exhausted.'' She yawned again, making a ceremony out of the movement. She really was tired, she realized. Wrecking cars and holding conversation with Thomas had completely drained her. "But thanks for bringing in the chest. I'd really like to just kick back and go to bed."

A lazy grin curled his mouth. "Sounds good to me. I could rub your back."

Rebecca silently chided herself for stepping into that one. Why did the one man she didn't want fawn all over her, and the one she did barely notice her?

Oh, he noticed you tonight, Bec. How could he miss when you smashed his eighty-five-thousand-dollar car? Or before that, when you almost ran over him? Or when you almost ran off the road into the hollow and killed him?

"Not tonight, Jerry. I don't want to keep you from your dinner plans."

"Uh, yeah." He rubbed his protruding belly. "I am kind of hungry. A man can't go without his food. And Pokey makes the best onion rings this side of the Chattahoochee." He slapped his chest. "Gives me gas, but all good things come with a price, right?"

"Right." She smiled sweetly, pushing images of him and chili and greasy onion rings out of her mind.

He dragged his feet toward the door. "Just let me know when you want to take a spin on my Hog, baby."

"I'm not really a Harley girl." Not that he actually had a Harley, anyway, although he told everyone he did; he had an *imitation* Harley.

He whistled through his teeth. "Just call me if you need anything."

Rebecca nodded and locked the door behind him, then changed into flannel pajamas. She did have several bruises on her chest, the skin was already turning an ugly purple. With a cup of hot chocolate in hand, she headed toward her bed when the hope chest drew her eye, beckoning her as if it had some kind of hypnotic spell on her.

Her heart fluttered with a tiny seed of hope. Hope that marriage and babies might be in her future. Curiosity gnawed at her, too, drawing her closer until she knelt beside the wooden chest.

Hannah and Mimi and Alison claimed their hope chests had held magical secrets regarding their futures. That the items Grammy Rose placed inside had something to do with the men they would marry.

Was there something inside her chest that hinted about a new man coming into her life? Something that would convince her that love would find its way into her future?

THOMAS HAD BARELY FALLEN asleep when the phone rang.

"This is Terrence McGee, Dr. Emerson." The man's breath sounded shaky. "I think Nora's in labor."

Thomas ran a hand through his hair and sat up. Nora was two weeks overdue, so her husband was most likely right. "She's having contractions?"

"Yeah, but they're not regular. Says her back's hurting."

"Back labor," Thomas said. And this was her third child so it would probably come quickly. "Get her to the hospital, Terrence. I'll meet you there."

"Her feet're swollen twice the normal size, Doc, and she says she's dizzy. I'm worried."

"She'll be fine." Thomas forced a calm to his voice that he didn't feel. "Just get her to the hospital and we'll take care of her and the baby. Everything will be all right."

He hung up, swung his legs over the side of the bed and grabbed his clothes. No time for a shower, so he jerked on khakis and socks, then hurried to the bathroom and splashed cold water on his face. He didn't want the McGee baby making its entrance without him. According to her file, Nora had had complications with the other two births. He sure as hell hoped this one went smoother.

Sugar Hill General was modern, but it still didn't have the advanced equipment that the big Atlanta hospitals did.

Buttoning his shirt as he went, he remembered the night his baby brother had died. His mother hadn't had the advantages of a big modern facility, either; maybe if she had, the doctors could have saved the baby. Thomas had been twelve, but the helplessness he'd felt had been mindboggling. A frisson of unease rippled through him as he drove to the hospital. He phoned the hospital to warn them to be prepared for an emergency. Better to prepare for the worst.

Someday maybe he would have a son of his own. A family to replace the one he'd lost long ago.

But not until he settled permanently into his career, moved to the city and achieved his goals. When he had a child, he wanted it to have all the advantages he and his brother hadn't. The latest in medical technology for starters.

And he would never have that in a small town like Sugar Hill.

REBECCA'S FINGERS TREMBLED as she opened the hope chest. Knowing that her grandmother had chosen the items inside especially for her brought tears to her eyes. Grammy Rose had been the only stable mother figure in her life ever since she was nine, when her mother had died.

She brushed her fingers over the soft velvet, the scent of cedar and her grandmother's rose potpourri clinging to the inside of the chest as if to remind her of its origin. She had seen the bride's book before but hadn't noticed the white envelope lying beside it. Her heart pounding with excitement, she opened the letter and began to read.

My dearest, darling Rebecca,

You are a very special granddaughter because you remind me so much of myself when I was your age. You were the first of Bert's daughters, the one who brought a deep love into his marriage that cemented the bond between him and your mother.

But you were the one who suffered the most when your mother died. Although your own heart was aching, you pushed your feelings aside to comfort your father and little sister in their sorrow.

You showed such strength that the rest of us gained courage from you. But when you retreated to that silent place where you grieved, you never quite came back.

Always steady and strong, dependable and caring, you are loyal and trusting to a fault. Believe in yourself now, Rebecca. Take time to nurture your own dreams and talents, and love yourself the way you love others.

I wish for you happiness, true love and a man who will give you all the joy a partner can.

Love you always,

Grammy Rose

P.S. Inside you will find something old, something new, something borrowed and something blue.

REBECCA WIPED A TEAR from her eye, then picked up the lacy bride's book and stroked a hand over the embossed silver bells. With a wistful sigh, she flipped the pages, imagining the blank white spaces filled with signatures of guests.

Guests at her own wedding.

Knowing she was being silly, she laid the book down and dug deeper into the chest. A blue garter lay nestled on top of a larger white envelope. She placed the garter around her wrist and opened the envelope, her mouth gaping when she found a blank marriage license inside. What in the world was Grammy doing putting a marriage license in there? Did she expect Rebecca to need one in a hurry?

A nervous bubble of laughter escaped her at the thought.

Occasionally Grammy did some wacky things, just as various other members of the Hartwell clan had been known to do. This obviously was one of them.

Next she thumbed through the book on dream analysis. What on earth would analyzing your dreams have to do with getting married?

The corner of a small children's book peeked out. *The Ugly Duckling.* Rebecca traced her finger over the picture of the little yellow duck on the front, then the beautiful white swan, thinking she had always been the duck, Suzanne the swan. But she smiled as she flipped the pages, memories of Grammy's voice reading the story to her night after night echoing in her mind. She had so loved the awkward little duck and had cheered the lonely creature on as he battled his way through the story. Hugging the book to her chest, she imagined reading it to her own child one day. Was that the reason Grammy had put it in the chest—did she foresee a baby in Rebecca's future?

A little boy or girl with dark-black hair and green eyes. A little boy who had an amazing similarity to Thomas Emerson.

What in heaven's name was she thinking?

Feeling foolish, she propped the book on the floor beside her and searched the hope chest, unearthing an antique comb, brush and mirror set. Grammy Rose's. She'd seen it on the antique dresser in the guest bedroom where Rebecca had slept as a child when she'd stayed overnight.

Sentiment squeezed at her chest as she slid the brush through her hair, remembering the times she'd done so at her grandmother's. She'd stood in front of the mirror for hours, brushing her hair, pretending she was Rapunzel with long, flowing, silky hair.

Pretending she was beautiful. That a handsome prince would rescue her from being imprisoned in the tower.

She raised the silver mirror and stared at her reflection.

No beauty there.

Oh, she wasn't bad to look at, she admitted. Even with wire-rimmed glasses, her eyes were a nice shade of blue, and her skin smooth and creamy. Her mouth wasn't bad, although her nose was a little too long, and the tiny freckles on her nose made her look about twelve years old. No, she definitely wasn't ugly. Besides, looks were more about what lay on the inside than the outside. She cared about others and had a good heart. But she just wasn't the beauty queen type. Or the type to attract and hold on to a man like Thomas.

She wasn't imprisoned in a lonely tower, either. She had a decent apartment, a good job, and her cousins lived close by. And Uncle Wiley.

Refusing to batter her self-esteem any longer, she placed the mirror and brush set back in the chest, her eyes narrowing when she found another book inside. Not a children's book, but a book of poetry.

She traced a finger over the worn leather binding, surprised at the title. "Passions." Blushing, she opened the book, her mouth dropping open when she noticed the pages filled with drawings of erotic love poses. A poem had been written beside each nude sketch.

Oh, my goodness. She flipped back to the title page and gasped at the sight of her grandmother's name printed inside.

Not only did the book belong to Grammy, but she had been one of the contributing artists and poets!

THOMAS PLACED BABY GIRL McGee in her mother's arms, his heart finally steadying after the harrowing delivery. When Nora had arrived, she was already fully dilated, but the baby hadn't dropped. It was also breech, and he'd tried to turn it, but the fetus had gone into distress, and he'd finally resorted to a C-section. A wise move, since she had had the cord wound around her neck at birth and hadn't been breathing.

Terrence had passed out and nearly fallen into Thomas as he'd given the baby oxygen.

"Thank you, Doctor," Nora said, tears seeping into her eyes. "She's beautiful."

Terrence shoved a hand through sweat-soaked hair, looking worse than his wife as she nestled the baby to nurse her.

Terrence curved an arm around his wife. "She looks like you, Norrie."

Thomas's throat closed. It never ceased to touch him when parents held their child for the first time. And it was nice to see the baby with two loving parents.

Miracles did exist.

Only, there hadn't been one for his family.

The day he'd lost a brother, his entire family had fallen apart. His mother had sunk into a deep postpartum depression and told his father she didn't want him around anymore. She didn't need him. His father had abandoned them both.

Later, when he was sixteen, his mother had died in an accident.

He pushed the painful thoughts aside. Thankfully, today, the technology at Sugar Hill had been sufficient.

"Congratulations, you two." Thomas patted Nora's shoulder. "You did great, Mom."

She squeezed his hand. "It may be our third, but she's just as special."

Thomas chuckled and left to offer them some privacy, his mood lifted by the closeness of the family. A closeness he'd missed out on when his father left. Although he admired single women who raised their kids alone, he intended to be there every minute, if or when he had a child.

SHOCK SURGED THROUGH Rebecca. Her seventy-four-year-old grandmother had written erotic poetry and drawn nude sketches of lovers intertwined? She almost shoved the book back inside the hope chest, but curiosity won out, and she scanned the first few pages. Grammy had always been a lively and modern character, but the seductive tone of the poems and the details of the drawings were more risqué than she could have imagined.

Oh, my, my, my…

She read the third poem, the erotic words conjuring visions of her and Thomas Emerson….

Before and after they'd strolled down the aisle.

A shiver rippled up her spine. There was no way she could try some of the poses. Could she?

Rattled, she shook off the images and hastily repacked the items in the hope chest, hoping to pack away the fantasies as well. No sense getting all starry-eyed just because her grandmother had sent her a few odd gifts.

Still, she carried visions to bed with her and in her dreams, they resurfaced.

Images of her and Thomas, their naked bodies tangled together, giving each other delight. Images of the two of them making love all through the night.

Images of the two of them having a child.

WHEN REBECCA WOKE the next morning, a soul-deep ache stirred within her. Moving slowly, she sat upright, wincing at the sharp pain in her chest and the stiffness in her muscles. She adjusted the pillow to prop herself up, then she lay back and considered her options.

She wanted a baby so badly. She had even before Mimi had gotten pregnant, but watching Mimi go through the pregnancy had raised all kinds of fantasies in Rebecca's mind. And seeing Mimi's little girl, Maggie Rose, had only deepened the desire for a child of her own. But she needed a man to get pregnant, and she didn't have a boyfriend or even a possibility of one in sight.

Unfortunately, the only man in the world she wanted to have a baby with was Thomas Emerson.

But he would never see her as anything but a klutz who'd demolished his Porsche and nearly killed him on the way home. Plus, he certainly didn't owe her a favor; she owed him.

Still, her biological clock was ticking away like a time bomb. And she had to face the fact that Sugar Hill wasn't exactly crawling with single, eligible bachelors.

Take time to nurture your own talents and dreams, Grammy had written.

Her dream was to have a family.

The book on dream analysis beckoned her from the hope chest. She jumped out of bed, brought it back and snuggled under the covers, skimming page after page, fascinated by the information.

Hmm, dreams sometimes relayed subconscious thoughts and desires.

She sat up straighter, feeling rejuvenated and more confident as an idea formed in her mind. Maybe there was something to this hope chest magic after all. Grammy had always been modern. Maybe it was time *she* stepped into the twenty-first century herself. Women didn't have to have husbands to have a child. She could have one by herself. She had a decent job running the bookstore, she was responsible, healthy, and she would love the baby unconditionally.

She'd taken care of Suzanne after their mother had died, so she knew she would make a good mother.

Yes, she was going to believe in herself, just the way Grammy Rose had suggested.

She'd have a baby on her own.

There was just one little problem—she needed sperm to get pregnant.

A headache pinched at her as she struggled over what to do. She could visit a sperm clinic and have in vitro fertilization.

Too impersonal. She'd never be able to go through with it. And she couldn't possibly tell her baby that she'd bought the sperm from a stranger, that she knew nothing of his father but what she'd learned from a computer file.

What about asking someone she knew to be a donor?

Jerry's enthusiastic face sprang to mind, but a shudder gripped her.

The dark-haired baby from her dreams haunted her mind.

Grammy had said to follow her dreams. Maybe the dream had been an omen.

And in her dream the baby had been Thomas's baby.

Maybe the dream meant that she was supposed to have Thomas's baby!

He was smart, intelligent, good-looking. If he donated sperm to father her child, she would know that the baby would be healthy, and she could assure her child that he or she had a great father. But how would she approach Thomas?

Should she try to seduce him?

Nervous laughter tickled her insides. She could barely talk to Thomas without making a fool of herself.

And asking him to sleep with her would be wa-a-ay too personal.

Although the mere thought sent a million delicious sensations curling in her belly.

Maybe…no, she couldn't.

But she could ask him to make a little personal donation. After all, he was an OB-GYN. He probably dealt with single women wanting babies all the time. He'd even commented that he admired single mothers. And the fact that he was an OB-GYN might prove to be a blessing. He probably already knew doctors who could perform the procedure, and she wouldn't have to seek help from virtual strangers.

She'd keep the arrangement simple, too. Once she was pregnant, he wouldn't be obligated or need to have any personal contact with her at all.

She twisted the sheets in her hands, her stomach convulsing in a thousand knots. Now she just had to summon up enough courage to discuss the baby plan with him. And she would, she promised herself, right after she phoned her insurance company to take care of paying for the damages to his wrecked car.

A wistful sigh escaped her, a twinge of sadness following. She wasn't settling for less than her dream, she assured herself as she climbed from bed and headed to the shower. She was simply facing reality. If she couldn't have Thomas, she could at least have his child. That would be enough.

A moment of trepidation hit her as she turned on the spray of water. What would Thomas think of the idea?

Chapter Four

In the early-morning sunlight the idea of asking Thomas Emerson to father her baby didn't seem quite so wonderful. In fact, the more Rebecca thought about asking him to *help* her with the baby plan, the more nauseous she became. By the time she'd walked the two blocks to the bookstore, her legs felt like rubber bands, and she suspected that if she actually ran into Thomas or even saw him on the street, she'd lose the muffin she'd finally managed to down for breakfast.

Why couldn't she be more like Suzanne?

Disgusted with herself, Rebecca rushed toward the Book Nook to open up. Maybe she'd talk to Mimi today and ask for some advice. Or she could browse the shelves for some good self-help books. Something on bolstering courage and acting with confidence. Or one on not acting like an idiot in front of men.

Could there possibly be a miracle book on talking without tripping over your tongue? Or flirting for the fainthearted?

Just as she reached the awning, she spotted Thomas driving by in a lemon-yellow Mustang convertible, obviously one of her uncle Wiley's loaners. A cold breeze suddenly stirred, sending leaves fluttering and her loose black skirt flying up around her legs. She tried to grab the billowing fabric, but it swirled up around her waist.

Nerves bunched in her stomach, and Rebecca panicked. Like a fool she swung around, ducked inside the door, crouched against a stack of magazines and pretended she hadn't seen him.

THOMAS FROWNED. He could have sworn Rebecca had seen him, but she'd ducked inside the bookstore as if she wanted to avoid him. Why?

After all, she'd left that hurried message on his answering machine saying she'd contacted her insurance company and her agent had assured her his car would be taken care of. He'd run from the shower, dripping wet, to reach the phone, but she'd babbled the message in seconds and hung up as if she was afraid she might actually have to talk to him. He'd simply wanted to assure her that he received the message.

Why was she avoiding him? Did she think he was a big ogre?

It wasn't as if he'd never been rejected before. He *had.* Dozens of times. Mostly because he'd always been Mr. Nice Guy, every girl's best friend or brother figure, and women liked the bad-boy types. Except, in this little town, the women had been especially friendly.

Of course, here pickings were slim. Half the townspeople had never left Sugar Hill. The half who'd stayed had married each other in high school and were now in the throes of mortgage payments, pregnancy, diapers, babies and small-town life with its lack of arts and entertainment. Either that or they were entrenched in divorce. Both comprised the population of his patients.

He wasn't sure which were more dangerous, the frustrated housewives, divorcées or hopeful singles faced with choosing mates from the same male pool they'd known since grade school. The limits of the small-town life.

Hormones and husband hunting were running rampant.

He waved to several patrons, chuckling at the raised eyebrows when they saw him driving the lemon-yellow car. Wiley Hartwell was a character, his used-car business a perfect extension of the outlandish man himself. What kind of man was his brother Bert?

From what he'd heard, he couldn't imagine the two men being at all similar.

Just like Rebecca and that sister of hers. Suzanne. The pretty brunette at the wedding.

Though Suzanne had a great pair of legs and would turn any man's head, something about Rebecca stayed with him.

Her innocence. She possessed a genuine sweetness that had been missing in most of the women he'd dated the past few years.

He ran a hand over his face, reminding himself not to start *caring* about her as he pulled into the clinic drive. He would be leaving soon. No time for attachments.

Taking a quick look at the Victorian house Hannah Hartwell had rented to house her practice, he couldn't help but mentally compare the old-fashioned structure to the modern women's center in Atlanta. Painted a pale yellow, the white gingerbread trim gave the Sugar Hill office a picturesque look, something his patients had commented on more than once. Patients claimed the building had a calming effect. Yet the cutting-edge technology and latest medical equipment and techniques in the modern facility in Atlanta were comforting in a different way. Medicine was about saving lives and the latest in technology, not hominess.

He parked in the shade, Wiley's reminders about the sunlight fading the new paint job on the Mustang rattling in his head, then grabbed his medical bag and hurried inside, hoping to clear his appointments by lunch so he'd have time to stop by the bookstore for a minute. If he intended to convince Rebecca to introduce him to her father, he'd have to do so soon. Her grandmother's surprise party was in just a few days. He couldn't let the opportunity slip by without doing something.

REBECCA SPENT THE MORNING tagging books for the after-Christmas sales and inventorying the results of the year's profits. The rush of women buying holiday craft books and cookbooks seemed endless. She'd half expected the women in Sugar Hill to be exhausted from baking for the various seasonal parties, but instead, they were planning New Year's Day dinners, Super Bowl get-togethers and church functions to collect food and clothing for the needy.

Mimi popped over with her baby, Maggie Rose. "Hey, Bec, you've been busy today."

"I know. Thank heavens. I'll need all the money I can get to pay my insurance premium now."

"You talked to your agent already?"

Rebecca nodded miserably. ''That had to be the worst day of my life.''

''How'd it go when you drove Thomas home after Alison's wedding?''

Rebecca cringed. ''Awful, Mimi. I'm such a klutz.''

Mimi squeezed her hand. ''Don't beat yourself up too much. Thomas handled the accident pretty well.''

''I suppose so. Then again, he is a nice man.''

Mimi laughed. ''Yeah, the nicest. Alison hated hurting him, but they weren't right for each other.''

''Do you think he's still in love with her?'' Rebecca asked.

''I don't think so.'' Mimi rocked Maggie Rose back and forth, and Rebecca's heart tugged at the tiny little fists sneaking their way out of the pink blanket.

Goodness, she wanted a baby so much.

Karina Peterson and Darlene Wilkerson, two girls her age, waltzed in a cloud of perfume and designer clothes.

Mimi rolled her eyes. ''Looks like those two have been dipping into their daddies' cash.''

Rebecca laughed. ''They've probably never worked a day in their lives.''

''I know. Listen, I need to run Maggie to Hannah's for a checkup.'' Mimi gestured toward the adjoining coffee shop. ''Bernadette and Angelina are running things, but I'll be back for the art class this afternoon. You're still having story time first?''

''Of course, my bag of puppets are ready.'' Rebecca tickled Maggie Rose under the chin, her heart touched by the angelic face staring up at her. ''She's so beautiful.''

Mimi tenderly kissed her daughter's forehead. ''I

know. And if I don't get going, Seth will be pacing the halls wondering why I'm late. That man's crazy about this kid."

Rebecca waved at her and returned to the register, fighting another bout of envy. The bell above the door tinkled and Bud and Red, two old-timers, loped toward the magazine rack for the latest wrestling magazine. A handful of teenagers milled around looking at teen magazines and comic books, already bored from the winter break.

Karina and Darlene browsed the sale area. "This spinach casserole looks fabulous," Karina cooed. "I'm going to cook it for Doc Emerson."

Rebecca froze at the cash register, her hand on the roll of quarters she needed for change.

"Isn't he the cutest thing to ever set foot in Sugar Hill?" Darlene said.

Karina giggled. "You bet your boots. I fabricated cramps last month just so I could sneak in an extra visit."

"Better watch out. I heard Trish Tieney is out to snag him. She told Elvira Baker that he's number one on her husband list."

"Drat. Trish does have those big boobs."

"And she's taking a French-cooking class."

Karina wrinkled her nose and reached for a book on desserts. "I know just the thing to win Dr. Emerson's heart—a double-chocolate layer fudge cake." She fanned her face. "Maybe I'll even dribble chocolate syrup on me and let him lick it off."

Rebecca coughed and dropped the roll of quarters she'd been opening, sending them rolling across the floor.

Both girls turned to glare at her, and she quickly stooped to pick up the change, pretending she hadn't heard their conversation. If beautiful Karina and Trish had their sights set on Thomas, she didn't have a chance.

She gathered the loose quarters and dumped them in the drawer. Karina watched her like a hawk as she rang up the purchases. ''Thanks, ladies,'' Rebecca said.

Feigning nonchalance, she wove her way to the self-help section, replaying her grandmother's words—*Believe in yourself. Follow your dreams.* But how could she do that when she acted like a simpering teenager at the mere thought of seeing Thomas?

She had to slay the dragon of self-doubt sitting on her shoulder.

Her eyes tracked the titles: *How To Be a Success in Business. Surviving Summers with Kids. Surviving Your Crazy Teenager. How To Master Menopause. How To Turn Up the Temperature in the Bedroom. The Art of Love.*

Unfortunately, she didn't see a single book with advice on how to ask a man for a sperm donation without stuttering.

MIMI JIGGLED MAGGIE ROSE up and down, trying to calm her after her vaccination.

''I'm so sorry,'' Hannah whispered, patting the baby's back. ''I didn't mean to make you cry, sugar.''

''It's all right,'' Mimi cajoled. She cradled Maggie Rose to her.

''You're a natural,'' Hannah said. ''Maggie Rose is lucky to have you for a mom.''

Mimi beamed. "She's my little doll baby. When are you and Jake going to take the plunge into parenthood?"

Hannah laughed. "We're working on it."

Mimi hugged her. "I hope you have an announcement soon. Maggie needs some cousins to play with."

"We'll see." Hannah tucked the blanket around Maggie Rose's feet. "Can you meet with Alison, Suzanne and Rebecca to plan Grammy's party?"

"Yep, Seth's going to watch the baby." Mimi grinned. "You know, Hannah, if my radar's working properly, Rebecca has a crush on Dr. Emerson. I think that's why she was so nervous and hit his car the other day."

"No big surprise." Hannah smiled. "Half the female population in town has a crush on Thomas."

Mimi scrunched her nose in thought, the wheels of mischief turning. "True, but if he marries anyone, it should be one of the Hartwell girls."

"He's on the rebound from a Hartwell now," Hannah pointed out.

Mimi shrugged. "But Rebecca is so sweet."

"And shy," Hannah said. "I wish we could do something to help her."

"You could talk her up to Thomas."

Hannah laughed. "I suppose I could."

"We need to figure out a way to get them together."

Hannah finished scribbling on Maggie's chart and closed it. "What are you scheming, Mimi?"

"Nothing much." Mimi grinned and surveyed the exam room. "Didn't you say you planned to hire someone to remodel the exam rooms?"

Hannah nodded.

"Well, I have an idea." Mimi wiggled her finger. "Let's go find Doc Emerson."

Hannah gave her a suspicious look. "I don't think we should interfere."

"Nonsense. Rebecca needs us." Mimi winked. "Just follow my lead, and wedding bells will be ringing for our cousin in no time."

"MY HUSBAND LEFT ME," Dorothy Parker wailed. "And I don't know what to do, Doc."

Thomas placed a comforting hand on Dorothy's back and slowly stroked, trying to calm her. She'd been crying for close to a half hour, which had sent her six-week-old infant into a fit, which had upset Dorothy even more. The two hysterical females had turned his routine follow-up exam into such a stressful ordeal he'd developed a raging headache.

At least now the high-strung woman was dressed and in his office.

Dorothy cradled the baby and leaned against him. "Harold left me for a waitress over at Crooked Neck Holler. Can you believe that? Just because I have a little baby fat left around my midriff."

Thomas refrained from commenting. "It takes time to lose weight after giving birth," he said softly.

"That's what I told him," Dorothy said, sniffing loudly. "But he said I'm not attractive anymore. Do you think he's right?"

A loaded question from a woman. Thomas pressed a finger to his temple. "New mothers are always beautiful, Dorothy, but stressed. I'm sure Harold will realize his mistake and come home soon. He'll be begging you to take him back.''

Her eyebrows lifted. ''Maybe I won't take him back this time.''

He stifled a comment; she and her husband split at least once a month. Harold had almost missed the delivery, because they'd had a whopping fight and he'd taken off to Ted's Tavern and gotten drunk. Cabs took a while to get from Atlanta to Sugar Hill.

''Maybe I'll just find someone else.'' Her tears dried, her eyes glinting with what he knew could be trouble. He moved aside to escape her clutches when a knock sounded at the door. Thankfully Hannah poked her head in and he slid from Dorothy's desperate grip.

''I...I was just leaving, Dr. Hartwell.'' Dorothy pulled herself together as Hannah and Mimi appeared in the doorway.

''Take care of that little one. I'll see you next year.'' At least, he hoped she wouldn't be back before her yearly exam. By then he would be gone.

Hannah raised a curious eyebrow, and Mimi giggled. ''Got your hands full?'' Hannah asked.

''You could say that. Did someone spray pheromones in the air?''

Mimi laughed. ''Now, there's a thought.''

''Do you have a minute?'' Hannah asked.

He nodded, although he'd planned to spend the next few minutes racking his brain on some way to approach Rebecca about her father.

''When I moved into the practice,'' Hannah said, ''I didn't have time to finish all the renovations. The exam rooms really need painting.''

''I can't argue with you there.''

''Mimi and I were talking, and she had a wonderful idea.''

He glanced at Mimi and the sleeping baby in her arms and smiled. Motherhood hadn't tamed the feisty redhead at all. In fact, she still wore gutsy clothes and kept the town talking, but Mimi was impossible not to like. ''I'm all ears.''

''I think you should have some pretty murals painted on the walls. Something calming to help patients relax.''

He nodded. ''You know someone who does that kind of work?''

''Yes, I do. She painted the sweetest mural of dancing teddy bears on the playroom wall for Maggie Rose.''

''She would be perfect,'' Hannah said.

''All right, you sold me. I hope she's local.''

''As a matter of fact she is,'' Mimi said excitedly. ''It's our cousin Rebecca.''

Thomas coughed. ''Rebecca's an artist?''

Mimi looked pleased with herself. ''Yep.''

''She paints beautiful landscapes,'' Hannah said.

''We think *you* should ask her,'' Mimi added with a devilish glint in her eyes.

''You do?'' Suspicion snaked in. ''Why?''

''Because we're related, and she never believes us when we brag about how talented she is,'' Mimi said. ''But if someone else does, she might believe it.''

He frowned, then wondered why he was even hesitating. This would be the perfect opportunity for him to get to know Rebecca better, to probe her about her father without being obvious about his intentions.

He'd be crazy not to jump at the chance they'd offered.

Maybe if she saw him at work, she'd realize he was basically a nice guy, not some temperamental jerk, and give him a good recommendation to her father.

Still, he'd have to walk a fine line. He couldn't become too involved with her. Friends, that's all they would be.

"All right," he agreed. "Maybe I'll run over to the bookstore at lunch and ask her."

"Great." Mimi lowered her voice. "Oh, but act like it was your idea. We don't want her to think we're interfering with her business."

"No," Hannah agreed. "We wouldn't want her to think that."

He nodded, although he wasn't quite sure they weren't interfering. But he had bigger things to worry about.

Like how Rebecca would react to his request. That is, if she didn't run the other way the minute she saw him.

Chapter Five

Haunted by the erotic words and images of her grandmother's poetry, Rebecca found herself meandering over to the small erotica section she housed in the far back corner and searching the titles and authors to see if her grandmother had contributed to any other selections. An artistic cover drew her eye, the colors a sultry hot pink and black, the title *Naughty-Rotica* drawn in a pale-pink shade of lipstick. She had just opened the book and skimmed the first entry, a very visual portrayal of a heated kiss drawn out with simple yet eloquent words, when someone cleared their throat behind her.

She turned, her jaw dropping open when she saw Thomas Emerson's intensely dark eyes fixed on her. His gaze lowered to the book in her hand, and something hot and seductive rippled through her. It was almost as if he had read the words on the page she'd been looking at and whispered them in her ear.

Ridiculous.

Men like Thomas didn't whisper naughty words or any kind of romanticisms to bookish girls like her.

Maybe she should reconsider her neighbor Jerry Ruthers.

His big belly flashed into her mind, though, and she winced.

"I saw you this morning when I drove past."

The sentence lingered in the strained silence between them. She could have just died.

Finally he saved her from her embarrassment. "I waved but I guess you didn't see me."

She could not even reply to that. "You…uh, received my message about the insurance?"

"Yes, I spoke with my agent, also. We'll work out the details."

She pushed her glasses up her nose. "Thanks for being so understanding."

He shrugged. "It was an accident. It's not like you did it on purpose."

"No, of course not."

Another strained silence fell between them. She didn't even try to fill the dead air for fear of stuttering. His gaze shifted to the book again, and she realized she had a death grip on it, so she shoved it back on the shelf. What in heaven's name was she doing?

"S-someone called in and as-sked about that book." She swung into motion and walked toward the phone at the front register. "I'll have to call them and let them know we have it in." *Dear lord, please let him believe that.*

The corner of his sexy mouth twitched into a lopsided smile. She cursed herself for noticing. "Did you n-need something? A book maybe?"

He shook his head. "Not a book. I need you, Rebecca."

She nearly tripped over a dump of paperbacks, a recent novelty called *Dating Disasters* that had climbed all the lists. They could have used her picture on the cover.

She took refuge behind the front desk, holding on to the laminated counter lest she completely lose her ability to stand. For pity's sake, that was what Thomas Emerson did to her.

''What did you say?''

Broad shoulders stretched against his crisp white shirt as he leaned on the counter to face her. ''I said I need you.''

I need you, too. At least your little swimmers.... ''Wh-why?''

The corner of his mouth twitched again. If she hadn't known better, she'd have thought he was flirting with her. How silly could she be?

''Hannah and I discussed fixing up the clinic. The exam rooms need painting, and I have it on good authority that you're a damn fine artist.''

''Oh.'' Of course he hadn't meant he *needed* her. He had his choice of women. ''Who told you I was an artist?''

''I'm a doctor, I treat half the town. They talk.''

Rebecca swallowed. ''But I don't make it a habit of sh-showing my work. I really just paint for m-me.''

His big hand reached over and slid on top of hers. The contact felt warm, comforting, yet it didn't comfort her at all. It aroused images of Thomas touching her. In places that she'd never allowed a man to touch her. In ways she'd seen sketched in that erotic book her Grammy had given her but had never experienced herself.

Except in her fantasies in the dark of night when she was alone.

"I can't." She shook off the disturbing images and pulled away, then began stacking new books that had arrived and needed shelving. Anything to keep her hands and mind occupied so they wouldn't stray into the danger zone.

"Why not? We'll pay you well."

"I..." She couldn't very well say she didn't need the extra money. After all, her insurance bill would skyrocket and he knew it.

"The place is pretty run-down. Yesterday, Ms. Hinkleman thought a crack in the ceiling was a spider and nearly broke her leg jumping off the exam table."

"Poor Ms. Hinkleman is ninety and half-blind."

"See my point. Consider it a service for the patients. You don't want them looking at peeling paint or freaking out while they have their exams."

Better that than his sexy face. "I...don't know. You've never even seen my work."

"You could invite me to your place and show me your drawings."

He *was* flirting with her.

She smiled in spite of her nerves. "I guess I do owe you, after crashing your car."

His smile faded slightly, then returned. "Yes, you do. Just help me out here and we'll call it even."

Rebecca swallowed. She did owe him. Worse, she wanted something from him, a favor much more personal than painting murals on a wall. How could she possibly turn him down and then ask him to help her have a baby?

IT WAS SO REFRESHING to talk to a woman who wanted nothing from him.

"All right," Rebecca said. "I'll d-do it."

"Good. Why don't we meet tomorrow after work and talk over some ideas. I'll get a crew to come in this weekend and put a fresh coat of primer on the walls, that is if I can find someone that fast."

Rebecca nodded, although she still didn't look comfortable with the idea. But at least she had agreed.

"Well, I'd better run. The s-storytelling hour."

He nodded again and watched as she rushed to the children's area to read to the kids. A twinge of guilt plucked at him for manipulating Rebecca into painting the clinic, but he dismissed it. She was such an innocent, giving to others without asking anything in return. Hadn't Hannah said that after Mimi had left?

Not like his mother, who'd only married his father to have a baby. Or half the women in town who wanted him to distract them from loveless marriages or make their husbands jealous by flirting with him. Or the debutantes back in Savannah who'd liked the fact that he was a doctor and thought by marrying him they'd automatically climb a step higher on the social ladder.

No, nothing would stop him from obtaining this new job or leaving town, especially a woman. He'd let Alison distract him momentarily, but he wouldn't put his heart on the line again only to have it crushed.

He owed it to the little brother he'd lost and to the family that had been torn apart because of it....

REBECCA RUSHED AWAY from Thomas so quickly she nearly slammed into Bud and Red.

"Whoa, darlin'." Bud grabbed her arms to steady her.

Red scratched at his scraggly beard. ''What's got you in such a tizz, Ms. Rebecca?''

Rebecca pushed her glasses back up on her nose. ''Sorry, fellas, I don't want to be late for children's hour.''

The old man nodded and released her. ''The young'uns all look forward to that.''

She smiled and smoothed down her skirt, then retrieved her bag of puppets and motioned to Gertrude, the girl who helped her part-time, to announce story time.

Five minutes later, she relaxed as the children huddled around her, hugging and whispering the stories they wanted to hear.

''Do the froggy song,'' three-year-old Cindy shouted.

''No, the train one, choo-choo, choo-choo.'' Five-year-old Andy pumped his arm up and down like the blare of a freight engine.

''We w-wanna hear 'bout the p-peanut butter monster.'' Six-year-old Lindy Sanders whispered in her stuttery voice. Every time the little girl stumbled over her sentences, Rebecca's heart lurched.

''We'll see if we have time for all those, I promise. But first, I'm going to tell you about a little bear who hibernated all winter.'' She slipped a fuzzy brown bear puppet from her bag and introduced him, then launched into the story. The children settled into the circle on the rug and stared wide-eyed as she told the story, her dramatics keeping them on edge as she described how the bear slept through Christmas, then finally emerged in the spring to find his mother giving birth to baby cubs. For the grand finale, she produced five small bear puppets and let the children name them.

Her heart swelled at the awe in the kids' eyes, and she took requests, making sure she used little Lindy's suggestion. She finished the hour with an audience-participation story, inviting the children to make the animal noises along with her as she sang ''Old MacDonald Had a Farm.'' Even Lindy forgot to stutter as she joined in the fun.

Afterward, she calmed them with a finger play before she sent them to Mimi for the follow-up art lesson they'd coordinated—they were cutting and pasting together bear puppets made out of paper plates. As the children hugged her goodbye, she pictured a child of her own, tucking him or her into bed at night, whispering a good-night story by the dim light of the moon glowing in the window. A little boy with black hair and grass-green eyes.

She looked up, half expecting to see Thomas Emerson watching her. She had to work up her courage to ask him about the baby plan.

But her nerve failed when she spotted him in Mimi's adjoining coffee shop. He wasn't alone. Trish Tieney had cozied up to him in a booth, flinging her wild red hair over her shoulder, giggling and flirting outrageously.

THOMAS TRIED TO FOCUS on Trish Tieney's long-winded diatribe about her real estate career; she had sold him his house, and no doubt he would need her services again when he decided to put it back on the market, but his gaze had strayed periodically to Rebecca and the show she performed for the children.

When she looked his way, he smiled, and she offered a strained one in return. Trish covered his hand with hers, and Rebecca turned away abruptly. Her easy dismissal of him stung.

Besides, she'd been so loving to all the kids, and she'd sung and told story after story with a dramatic flair, and hadn't stuttered once with them.

"If you need furniture, I'd be glad to go shopping with you," Trish offered. "I minored in decorating at Valdosta State."

"I'm fine for now," he said, knowing he didn't want to buy anything else that might not fit into his new place. But he was getting ahead of himself. He still had to land the job.

"The invitation's always open." She flipped her curly hair over her shoulder for about the dozenth time. She must think the gesture was sexy but it simply annoyed him.

"Thanks, I'll keep that in mind." He stood and pushed his chair back. "I have to get back to the clinic now."

Trish raked fake red nails down his arm. "If you need anything else, too, just give me a call. I'd be glad to cook you a French dinner one night."

"Uh...sure, that sounds great." What else could he say?

He rushed toward the door, but he couldn't help himself. He turned and searched the bookstore one more time for Rebecca. But she was helping a customer, some burly guy who needed a shave, and she didn't even glance his way.

"LISTEN, JERRY, I appreciate the invitation," Rebecca said, "but I'm not much of a dancer."

"Aww, come on, Becky, the American Legion plays great country music. And it's New Year's Eve, everybody'll be there." He waggled his eyebrows. "I'll teach you the two-step. It's real easy." He leaned forward, so close his burgeoning belly brushed her arm. "It'll give us time to scrooch up and get to know each other better."

Exactly what she didn't want. "I...I think..." *I'll have a headache that night.* "I'll let you know."

He grinned toothily as if he'd just won the lottery, tugged his baggy jeans up by the loops, then whistled. "Guess I'd better get back to work. Got to butcher two hogs this afternoon."

Rebecca nodded, chastising herself for giving him even a smidgen of hope. Why hadn't she just said no? *Me and you scrooching or doing anything else that involves touching is not going to happen. I can't imagine letting your smelly hands hold me, especially knowing you've been cutting up pig's guts with them.*

Furious with herself for being such a wimp, she jogged back to the self-help section. She'd find a book on being assertive and learn a few techniques on handling herself better. Because she'd rather die than have Jerry's belly brushing hers all night long. And, God forbid, it would be worse to let him think she liked it.

Then he would never leave her alone.

BY THE END OF THE DAY Thomas had two chicken casseroles, a sweet potato custard and two jars of homemade peach preserves to cart home with him, all compliments of the single women of Sugar Hill. Their mothers must have taught them that the way to a man's heart was through his stomach.

But something else worked just as well. Only, none of the women seemed to spark an interest in him in that area.

None except Rebecca Hartwell, who seemed immune to his charms.

Granted the food smelled great, and he hadn't wanted for a single meal since he'd moved here, but this was getting ridiculous, as was the sudden increase in women's ailments. Karina Peterson had dropped by complaining of a nonexistent pain in her side—he was beginning to think the woman was a hypochondriac. Then her friend Jillie Flannigan, who'd been in the week before with a similar ailment, had invited him to her daughter's piano recital, hinting that her little girl needed a father figure.

He packed the food in the back of the Mustang and drove the short distance to his house, the cool December breeze blowing leaves and twigs across the road. The bare trees swayed with the wind, the threat of rain scenting the air as he went inside the house. He heated up one of the chicken casseroles, then scooped a helping on his plate and set up his laptop, but the house felt unusually quiet tonight. The massive furniture seemed more massive, the gleaming floors shiny but silent, lacking friendly footsteps, the perfectly decorated walls devoid of life. He tried to remember what kind of paintings he had on the walls, but he couldn't visualize any particular one. What kind of artwork did Rebecca like? Did she choose soft colors or flashy neon shades or vibrant purples and blues that signified passion?

He could not think about passion and shy Rebecca Hartwell in the same second.

His thoughts drifted to Trish Tieney and Karina Peterson and the way they'd both flirted with him today, then to Rebecca Hartwell and how she'd practically avoided him.

Like it or not, she would see him tomorrow.

He ignored the small flutter of desire that curled in his belly at the thought of spending time with her. Sure, he was a red-blooded male and he had to admit she was attractive. But she was not the bed-'em-and-shed-'em type. And he couldn't start something that would go nowhere. End of story.

He forced himself to eat and block Rebecca and those blue eyes from his mind.

Of course, the other women who'd brought him food today might give him a one-night stand, but he couldn't accept. Another downside to small towns was that if he slept with a woman, it was bound to get around town. And he would never sleep with one of his patients.

All the more reason he needed to move.

He scanned the data on the Atlanta medical facility, jotting notes about the plans for the research facilities and surgical specialities they planned to offer, along with the fertility clinic that would be housed inside. Maybe he'd check out Atlanta housing while he was at it. The sooner he nailed down his plans, the better. Then he could finally have the life he wanted....

Chapter Six

The crisp winter air smelled heavenly as Rebecca left the Book Nook to go home to her apartment. She'd rented one of the small lofts the town had recently renovated to encourage newcomers, and loved it. The small loving town had embraced her like the arms of one of the ancient oaks and become her extended family, offering her a comforting haven through friends and family.

She'd moved around all the time when she was young, never having a real home. She couldn't imagine ever leaving or living anywhere but Sugar Hill.

Although some of the downtown area still needed a facelift, and a few shops were struggling, Mimi's shop and hers were successful, and so was Alison's bridal boutique, Weddings To Remember. She passed her aunt's law practice, the antique store, Cissy's Cut and Curl, and a hardware store. Roger Thornhill had a small feed store, and Wilbur Cummings had opened a hobby shop across the way where the kids exchanged baseball cards and the men met for checkers. Beside the bakery sat the butcher shop where Jerry worked; she always avoided it on the way home. The town had also added a playground in the center of the square with benches for the moms and dads to relax.

She darted inside the florist's, gazing at the roses in the window along with the other assorted flowers and plants, memorizing the details of each one to add to the painting she'd started of her grandmother's flower garden. Enchanted by the heavenly scents, she couldn't resist; she bought a bouquet of assorted flowers to take home.

As she stepped outside, a gust of wind rustled the elms and maples and spun the weather vane that topped the hardware store. Neon-green and orange signs advertising her uncle Wiley's end-of-the-year used-car sale swung back and forth above the one stop light in the town square. He'd also run radio commercials advertising the special extravaganza on New Year's Eve, featuring live entertainment with an Elvis Presley impersonator scheduled to sing before Wiley gave away a car—a 1945 pickup he'd custom painted purple. Uncle Wiley was such a character, so easy to talk to that you had to love him.

Except, he and her father didn't get along at all. She'd never quite understood what had caused the rift between them. Her dad complained about Uncle Wiley's outrageous ads, called him cheesy and said he was an embarrassment to the family. Wiley claimed her father was a snob, that he'd turned his back on his family when he'd moved to Atlanta.

Maybe they would behave themselves at Grammy's surprise party. She certainly hoped so.

Rebecca rounded the corner to her apartment and opened the wrought-iron gate, then froze. She heard Jerry before she saw him, his muffler roaring above the strains of Garth Brooks's ''Shameless'' bellowing from the speakers. No matter what time of year, Jerry kept his windows rolled down.

Not wanting to face him tonight, she sprinted inside before he gathered his thermos and lunch pail and locked up his truck. Once inside, she ignored his phone call. Thank heavens for caller ID. After a week of him knocking at her door unannounced, she'd learned to keep her music low and her shades drawn. Then he never knew if she was home or simply ignoring him.

It was easier than hurting his feelings.

She fixed herself a sandwich, then changed into her grubby clothes and went to the easel. She'd already completed one canvas of her grandmother's bulb garden—the white, crimson and yellow tulips and blue hyacinths set off by the wide, sweeping border of purple Virginian stock. This time she decided to paint the mountainscape and detail the gazebo where her cousins had married; it would be her birthday present to Grammy.

The next two hours Rebecca lost herself in her work, mixing colors and painting details of the lush mountain greenery, then filling the mountainside with day lilies and wildflowers. At last her eyes were so heavy, she put the paints away and settled down to bed. The hope chest glinted in the dim light of the Victorian lamp on her bedside table, the items beckoning. She reread her grandmother's letter, each carefully chosen word etched into her memory. Then she raised the antique mirror to study herself.

Follow your dreams. Believe in yourself.

She whispered the words over and over in her mind.

The book of erotic poetry beckoned her, but she refused to torture herself with the fantasies they evoked of a night in a man's loving arms.

Of a night with Thomas.

Instead, she crawled into bed and closed her eyes. That dream would never come true. But maybe the other one would.

During the night, she dreamed that the sweet scent of an acacia drifted around her. Its soft branches were clothed in pointed, silvery, evergreen leaves, the thick double pom-poms of fragrant bright-yellow blossoms in full bloom.

The next morning she checked the dream analysis book to see if it mentioned dreaming of flowers, acacia especially. She found a reference on the third page.

Acacia—to see it bloom or smell its fragrance is a lucky omen for your most secret hope, your passion.

Could it be possible? Would her secret hope of having a baby come true?

Or did it mean that she might find the passion she hoped for with a man?

"REBECCA!" SUZANNE WAVED. "Glad you met us."

Rebecca claimed the vacant seat beside Suzanne. All the girls had met outside town at a small café called Ms. Mabel's. Mimi and Hannah were already seated with coffee. "Hey, sorry I'm a little late. I got tied up with customers."

"It's been wild at the Hot Spot this morning, too," Mimi said. "I'm glad we could meet here or else I'd be having to get up to help out."

"Have you heard from Alison?" Suzanne asked.

"They're enjoying their honeymoon." Hannah grinned. "I've never heard Alison so happy."

"Newlywed bliss," Mimi said dreamily.

A seed of envy sprouted inside Rebecca. "Will she be back for Grammy's party?"

"Yes," Hannah said. "That's one reason we decided to wait until after New Year's."

"Okay, what do we need to do to get ready for the party?" Suzanne asked.

Mimi pulled out her planning book, and Hannah did the same.

"We're having the festivities at a little place called the Tiara Room near Pine Mountain. They've reserved a room for us in the back and will provide all the food."

"Except for the cake," Mimi said, "which I'll make."

"Do they have a real tiara there?" Rebecca asked.

"Apparently, they showcase one for each of their Little Miss Magnolia pageants along with pictures of the yearly winners." Mimi gestured toward the top of her head. "Maybe I'll buy one while I'm there. Then Seth will know I'm queen of the house."

"I'm sure he's learned that by now," Hannah said dryly.

The girls all laughed.

"Grammy's friend, Clara Mae Wilkins, has commandeered a church bus to bring all of Grammy's friends," Hannah said as their laughter died down.

"Good, I was afraid they wouldn't be able to attend," Rebecca said. "I know most of them don't drive."

"Right." Hannah tapped her notepad with her pen.

"Clara Mae has already laid the groundwork for the surprise by inventing a bingo outing near the Tiara Room so Grammy won't be suspicious."

"Now that we've figured out how to get Grammy to the surprise, what are we going to do about getting our fathers there?" Hannah asked.

Mimi leaned her chin on her hand. "I don't understand this rift between Dad and Uncle Bert. Brothers should be close, like we are."

Hannah squeezed Mimi's hand. "I know, it's a shame."

"It sure is." Suzanne sighed. "I'll do my best to convince Dad he has to come." Suzanne turned to Rebecca. "You should call him, too, sis."

"He listens to you more than me."

Suzanne's eyes narrowed into a frown, her gaze meeting Rebecca's. She knew their father favored her, didn't she? Or was she oblivious to the tension between Rebecca and their dad?

"I'm sure he wants to see you, Bec." Suzanne's voice sounded so sincere. "I just hope he and Uncle Wiley can be in the same room without slitting each other's throats."

"Maybe we should tell each of them that the other one won't be there," Mimi suggested.

Hannah made a skeptical face. "That might backfire and fireworks could explode."

Rebecca imagined the scene. "I agree. I think we should prepare them."

"But let's issue strict orders that they can't fight," Hannah said.

"They definitely have to behave," Mimi said. "We don't want anyone to ruin Grammy's party."

"I'll see if we can't find Aunt Shelby, too," Hannah said. "No one in the family has heard from her in ages, but I'm sure Grammy wants her there."

"It'll be like a big family reunion!" Mimi squealed. "And Maggie Rose is starting a new generation of Hartwell girls. Maybe Hannah and Alison will add to the crew by next year."

The girls laughed, but Rebecca remained silent, her own desire for a baby mounting.

She was thankful when the food arrived, and the girls dug into salads, quiches and soup. "This is divine," Suzanne said. "It reminds me of a neat little café in a hotel near Little Five Points."

"Speaking of hotels," Mimi said, clapping the table. "There's a small place adjoining the Tiara Room called the Honeysuckle Inn for anyone who wants to stay over and not drive back that night." Mimi winked. "Seth and I are looking forward to spending a romantic night there."

"Jake and I plan to stay over, too," Hannah said with a grin. "I can't wait to have him all to myself, no phone calls, no emergencies for either one of us."

"You two can bring a date," Mimi offered.

Thomas's face materialized in Rebecca's mind, but she quickly banished it. Not only would he *not* want to attend a family birthday party with her, but Alison and Brady would be there, fresh from their honeymoon. If he still harbored feelings for her cousin, seeing the newlyweds would only rub salt into his wounds.

"I might bring someone," Suzanne said. "I have been dating this hot guy named Nick."

Rebecca winced. Of course Suzanne would have a great guy to escort her.

And like high school, *she* would be the wallflower.

As soon as the girls went their separate ways, Mimi pulled Hannah to the side. "Did you see Rebecca's face when you mentioned a date?"

Hannah nodded. "Yeah, she looked kind of dreamy, then sad."

"I bet she was thinking about Thomas."

"We don't know for sure. Maybe there's someone else...."

"You didn't see her tortured expression when she asked me if I thought he was still in love with Alison."

"That bad, huh?" Hannah asked.

Mimi nodded. "Downright pathetic. We have to give them a nudge."

"But what if he isn't interested?"

Mimi thumped her fingernail on her chin. "Feel him out this afternoon, okay?"

Hannah rolled her eyes. "All right, but I just hope he doesn't catch on. I don't want him to think I'm interfering in his personal life."

Mimi laughed. "Honey, men need a little interference or else they'd all stay single forever."

Hannah chuckled, and Mimi grabbed her arm and walked with her to the door. "You work on him and I'll work on Rebecca. Maybe we can talk her into a shopping trip. I'll discuss it with Suzanne. We need to swap those baggy clothes for some sexy ones, so he can see her great figure.''

THOMAS ESCORTED Rachel Lackey to the door. ''Now remember, call me anytime if you start having contractions.''

''Thanks, Dr. Emerson.'' Rachel laid a hand over her burgeoning belly. ''I don't know what little Rodney and I would do without you.''

He shrugged. ''Just doing my job.''

Rachel waved and left. Thomas sighed, grateful she had a husband. His last patient, Benita Waters, had asked him to dinner right in the middle of her exam. He'd been stunned and had resorted to his usual line—he didn't date his patients.

Afterward, he'd heard Benita tell Hannah to switch her patient file to Hannah for her next exam.

''Ready to call it a day?'' Hannah asked.

''Yes, how about you?''

''I just finished with the Terrel twins. What a handful.''

He laughed. ''Doesn't make you want a kid?''

''Not like those two. They're holy terrors.'' She slid the chart in the bin to be filed. ''What happened with Benita? I thought she loved having you as her doctor.''

He grimaced and explained the situation.

''So you suggested she see me from now on so you could date her?'' Hannah asked.

''No.'' Thomas raked a hand through his hair. ''I don't intend to date her. Coming to you was her idea. Sorry about that.''

''It's not your fault every single woman in town wants you.''

He chuckled. ''Actually, not every one does.''

She offered a teasing smile. ''Someone turn you down for a date?''

''Not exactly.'' He shifted, fumbling with a file, unsure whether to confess. But, hell, what harm could it do? ''Your cousin Rebecca seems less than enthusiastic about being around me.''

''Hmm. Did you ask her about the murals?''

''Yes, and she agreed. Reluctantly. I don't know what I've done to make her uncomfortable, but I got the distinct impression she doesn't like me.'' And that really bugged him.

Hannah laughed. ''Then I guess you'd better turn on the charm when she comes to paint the murals.''

He shrugged, then remembered the lunch meeting to plan the party for her grandmother. ''How'd the planning session go today?''

''Great. We nailed down the details.'' She described the Tiara Room and the small inn where guests would probably stay. ''Oh, and Mimi mentioned to Suzanne that she and Rebecca could bring dates.''

''Really.'' Why did that idea bring a twinge of jealousy?

''Suzanne already has someone in mind,'' Hannah said. ''I'm not sure about Rebecca, though. It'll be interesting to see who she brings. It'll take a special man to see through her shyness to the wonderful person inside.''

He saw through her shyness.

And he'd better be her date, he thought, irritated with Hannah's comment, although he didn't take the time to analyze the reason. Wasn't he special enough for Rebecca?

He grabbed his doctor's bag and headed to the door to firm up plans about the paintings. But he decided to take Hannah's advice and turn on the charm, just in case he had competition.

Not that he really *wanted* a date, he reminded himself. But he did want to attend that party—to meet her father. Nothing more.

REBECCA STEELED HERSELF for her meeting with Thomas. In fact, she'd been reading *How To Get What You Want* in between customers, practicing the visualizing techniques they suggested for thinking yourself into success. But whenever she'd imagined herself turning him on with just one passionate look, enticing him to make love to her to get her pregnant instead of donating his sperm into a plastic vial, visions of her stuttering and falling on her face in front of him had slipped in. She paced the sidewalk in front of the store where they were supposed to meet. Thinking the fresh air would relax her, she'd suggested they walk to the courtyard park in the square. Unfortunately, it was starting to drizzle, and the wind had whipped up something fierce.

Why, oh, why had she agreed to do this?

She glanced along the sidewalk but didn't spot him, then heard a horn and saw the lemon-yellow Mustang drive up in front of the store. "It's starting to rain. Get in."

She swallowed hard, remembering the last time they'd ridden together, when she'd driven like a maniac and almost killed him.

"Come on, Rebecca, I won't bite."

His sexy, teasing grin did nothing to relax her. But how could she argue?

She slid inside the car and fastened her seat belt.

"Let's talk over dinner."

"D-dinner?"

"Yes, you do eat, don't you?"

She nodded. But dinner seemed too much like a date.

"Then let's go. I know this great little place outside town. Then we can skip back to your place."

"M-my place?" Heavens, that would be way too intimate.

You want to have this man's baby, Rebecca. For God's sake, how do you think you'll ask him to do that if you can't even let him come to your apartment?

Chapter Seven

Thomas's shoulders ached as he drove to the restaurant. Rebecca was holding on to her seat with a death grip, as if she expected him to jump her bones any minute.

He'd glimpsed a few very nice curves beneath that denim skirt when she'd climbed into the car. Her breasts had swayed and dipped enticingly, stirring his arousal. And her scent, some kind of light flowery fragrance, was driving him wild. He turned on the radio to a soft rock station to fill the strained silence and tried to regain his equilibrium. Rebecca Hartwell was not supposed to affect him this way. Good grief, he saw dozens of women all day long, and not one Sugar Hill resident stirred his hormones like Rebecca.

Conversation. He should get her talking to thwart this insane reaction his body seemed to be having. "What kind of music do you like?"

She cleared her throat. "Just about everything. Oh, except for rap and hard rock."

"Favorite?"

"Country."

He hated country. "Do you like to work out?"

She shrugged. "I walk back and forth to work every day."

He wasn't exactly a fitness fanatic but he liked to keep in shape. "I have a gym—" At home, he almost said, but he didn't want to sound as if he was bragging. "I joined."

She didn't comment.

"How about sports? You follow any of the major league teams?"

"B-baseball."

"Yeah, I keep up with the Braves. But I love football."

She shuddered. She obviously hated it. "My d-dad is glued to the set on Sundays."

So was he, but she didn't sound as if she approved. "Do you like outdoor activities? Hiking, camping, boating? Skiing?"

"I'm not very athletic. I m-mostly like art and books."

Did they have *anything* in common? "I hope you like eclectic food."

"I'm easy to please."

He wished!

Another strained silence fell between them. He'd never had this much trouble talking to a woman before in his life. Which proved that he certainly had no business getting involved with Rebecca.

Grateful when the restaurant appeared, he filled the next few minutes as he parked detailing the menu. He knew it by rote, everything except for the nightly specials.

A sigh of disgust lodged in his throat. He sounded like a waiter.

"You must come here a lot," Rebecca said as she opened the car door.

"Yeah. But I have enough casseroles from the ladies so I don't have to eat out every night."

She frowned and he wished he hadn't mentioned the casseroles. He scooted out and hurried around to help her, but she had already stood and closed the door. Probably didn't want to have contact with him. Did she think he had leprosy or something?

"This way." He placed his hand at the back of her waist, well aware she tensed when he did so, but he didn't care. Dammit, he was just trying to be nice. The Southern gentleman his grandma raised him to be. The kind all the Savannah debutantes would have expected. Yet Rebecca seemed to have no expectations.

Or desire for him, either.

The maître d' seated them at a small table in the corner. The lighting was dim, the spicy aroma filling the room with delicious odors, the soft strains of violin music adding to the ambience.

"It smells wonderful." Rebecca took the menu and studied it, chewing on her lip.

"May I get you some drinks?" the waiter asked.

"W-water," Rebecca said.

"I'll have unsweetened iced tea. And let me see the wine list." He opened it and scanned the selections, naming a few for Rebecca to choose from.

"Wine's not n-necessary," she said.

Irritation flitted through him. "Rebecca, we're just going to have a glass. I'm not trying to seduce you, so you can relax."

"I didn't mean to imply you were. I mean, I'm sure you wouldn't do such a thing."

Did the idea of him seducing her disgust her so much? He exhaled noisily. "What do you mean?"

"I..." She dropped her head forward, that long, blond hair spilling down like a silky curtain. "You...you and I. It's silly."

Anger deepened his voice. "What's so silly about it? And why are you avoiding me?" Had he really blurted that out?

She gaped at him, her big blue eyes enormous beneath those glasses. "I...who said I was avoiding you?"

"It sure seems that way."

"I'm sorry."

"Stop apologizing."

"You don't have to raise your voice."

He closed his eyes and reined in a temper he didn't even know he possessed. When he opened them, she was watching him warily. He swore he saw the beginning of a tear in her eye and felt as if he'd just kicked a puppy.

"I'm sorry. I don't know what's gotten into me." *Literally.* Suddenly hot, he tugged at his collar, then instinctively reached out and covered her hand with his. She felt delicate and soft, a warmth radiating from her hand to his. He'd never been claustrophobic, but he suddenly felt closed in. At the same time he contemplated what it would feel like to pull her in his arms. "I guess I misunderstood. You've been so standoffish I thought you disliked me."

A whispery breath escaped her. "It's not that. I just know you wouldn't try to seduce a girl like me."

Was she crazy? "And why not?"

Her eyelashes fluttered. ‘‘We...have nothing in common.’’

‘‘Sometimes opposites attract.’’

‘‘But you’re outgoing. I’m too sh-shy. Too quiet. Bookish.’’

‘‘I like books. And quiet people are good listeners.’’

A small smile curved her pink lips.

‘‘Besides, we’re just talking about being friends,’’ he said, determined to put her at ease. He didn’t want to seduce her. Did he?

‘‘Right.’’

Was that disappointment lacing her voice? He studied her, trying to read her reaction, but the waiter interrupted, and he ordered two glasses of Merlot. She chose a northern Italian salmon pasta with artichoke hearts and he ordered the steak and lobster.

After the waiter brought their drinks, he raised his glass, but his hand trembled just as it had the first time he’d entered a delivery room, which was ridiculous. Seeing Rebecca was nothing like taking his first giant step into medicine. ‘‘Can we start over?’’

She nodded and met his gaze. This time her vibrant blue eyes sparkled with interest, and his belly tightened.

‘‘To f-friendship.’’

She clinked his glass. ‘‘To f-friendship.’’

‘‘And to art.’’

She laughed softly this time. ‘‘I can’t believe you hired me and you haven’t even seen my work. I normally don’t show it to strangers.’’

‘‘Then I’ll be honored,’’ he said honestly.

‘‘Really, you didn’t have to take the time to do this. I could work out the arrangement with Hannah.’’

She would like that, wouldn't she? Another dodging maneuver.

"No need for that." He covered her hand with his again. "I think we'll work together just fine, Rebecca."

REBECCA FINALLY RELAXED and managed to string together a few complete sentences rather than the monosyllabic answers she'd produced in the car—at least enough to get him talking about his family.

Yet, she still lapsed into wondering why any man would want her. Talk about uninteresting. She wasn't athletic. Didn't like sports. Just art and books.

She might as well brand the word *boring* on her forehead!

"So, I'm an only child," his voice grew low as he finished. "I lost the one brother at birth, I think I mentioned him to you before. I was twelve but I'll never forget the day he died."

"I'm so sorry." He looked so desolate for a second, she laid her hand over his.

He curled his fingers into hers for a brief second and squeezed gently, sending a current of delicious sensations spiraling through her. A bead of perspiration gathered inside her dress and rolled into her bra. Gracious, the man did things to her.

Then he pulled away and sipped his glass of wine. "Tell me about your family. You have the one sister, that's all?"

"Yep, just me and Suzanne."

"She lives in Atlanta?"

"Y-yes." Darn it, there she went stuttering again. All because they were talking about her gorgeous sister. ‘‘She works for a land development company.’’ And likes to ski and go to the gym.

Maybe she should fix the two of them up.

Heaven help her, what could she be thinking?

‘‘Are you close to your father?’’

Rebecca shrugged and toyed with her napkin. ‘‘We don’t talk a lot. He’s busy with his new wife.’’

‘‘You seem close to Hannah and Mimi and Alison.’’

‘‘I am.’’ Rebecca smiled, thinking how her cousins had always drawn her in to their group. Was he wishing Alison was sitting across the table from him?

He stretched back while the waiter took their plates, then ordered coffee for both of them. Seconds later the rich, dark brew was delivered.

‘‘I lined up the crew to paint. We’re closing the clinic on the twenty-eighth, so hopefully the grunt work will be completed before New Year’s. Maybe you can start right after that.’’

‘‘Sure. I have inventory at the bookstore, but my assistant can handle that. Do you have anything specific in mind for the murals?’’

‘‘I was hoping you did. I’m not very creative.’’

Rebecca stirred sweetener into her coffee. ‘‘I normally paint landscapes. I’ve done a few children’s murals, too.’’

‘‘Mimi was excited about the one you did for Maggie Rose.’’

‘‘That was my baby present to her.’’

‘‘She loved it. It was an animal scene, right?’’

She nodded. ‘‘Actually, I have been thinking of a few ideas.’’

‘‘I’m all yours—’’ he snapped his head up ‘‘—I mean, all ears.’’

She laughed. Of course he hadn't meant that, although the words conjured up fascinating images. "How many exam rooms are there?"

"Six. Normally I use three, Hannah uses the other three for her family practice."

"All right. I could paint some landscape or floral scenes in the adult rooms, maybe a garden scene or the mountains in the winter. Then I'll do a couple of murals for kids in the family exam rooms. Maybe a zoo scene and a dinosaur one. Those are universally popular with kids."

He nodded. "That sounds great. We could even designate the rooms with a name for each scene."

Excitement swelled in Rebecca's chest. As they left the restaurant, she gave herself a silent pat on the back for surviving dinner without making a fool of herself.

Still, she hadn't broached the subject of the baby plan. Maybe when she got to know him just a little bit better....

She absolutely couldn't let herself fall for him, though. After all, they had nothing in common. In fact, in some ways he reminded her of her father—his job, his interests, his ambition.

She could never be with someone as driven as her dad. His work required cocktail parties and business dinners, the very reason he always wanted some sophisticated woman by his side...and the reason Suzanne was his favorite. She handled social events like a professional hostess. Her father's house was gigantic, formally decorated with modern sculptures and pristine white walls, not at all a welcoming home for a family or children. It was more of an entertainment palace.

Would Thomas want that kind of life one day, too? A wife to help him entertain colleagues and throw dinner parties for the hospital board. He was so intelligent. Would he be satisfied to stay a small-town doctor forever?

Or would he leave Sugar Hill one day to pursue bigger things, as her father had done?

THOMAS FOLLOWED REBECCA up the stairs to her flat, admiring the colorful pansies in the window boxes and the country-style, woodcrafted welcome sign on the front door. A beefy guy wearing grubby jeans yelled from below, ''Yo, Becky.''

Rebecca tensed and pivoted to glance down the stairway, then offered the man a small wave.

''New Year's is still lookin' good.''

''We'll talk later.'' She fumbled with the key, then rushed inside.

He swung another look at the guy below before he stepped into the apartment, wondering at his relationship with Rebecca. But since she didn't comment, he decided not to pry. If the man was her boyfriend, why should he care? After all, he would be leaving soon, right?

The entryway of her apartment showcased antiques and homemade craft items with cross-stitch samplers and a collection of small wooden birdhouses in blues and yellows. Books overflowed an oak bookcase, while photos of her family lined one wall. An eight-by-ten of Rebecca with her father and sister sat on a table behind a Victorian sofa. Rebecca must have been about twelve in the photo, her sister a couple of years younger. She was scrawny and wore baggy clothes and her glasses, a picture of innocence and youth. But his heart tugged slightly at the sadness in her smile. Her father looked big and burly next to her, a powerful figure for such a dainty little child. He had his arm around both girls but his smile seemed aimed toward Suzanne.

"My loft isn't very big," Rebecca said, "but I like it here."

"It's cozy," he said. "A real home."

The very opposite of his showy, modern house.

And what were those delicious smells? Brownies? Apples and cinnamon maybe? It felt as if he'd just stepped into his grandmother's house.

Except Rebecca did not remind him of his grandmother in any way. Maybe the glasses, but behind those wire rims lay the sexiest blue eyes he'd ever seen.

Since when had he associated the word sexy with Rebecca?

Sweet, attractive, maybe, but sexy?

"My studio's in the spare room. It's small, too, but the lighting is good."

He passed the adjoining kitchen, then another room, which was obviously Rebecca's bedroom. A handmade quilt topped an antique white iron bed with dozens of pillows piled near the headboard.

He tried not to imagine Rebecca in that bed, but the image floated to him anyway. Her lounging against the pillows, looking at him with hunger in her eyes.

Thankfully, she couldn't tell his mind was wandering. In fact, she'd practically flown past the room and was already standing in the doorway of the studio. Small was right. The studio would only fill half of the walk-in closet in his master suite, but natural light spilled in through a skylight, and the ten-foot ceiling added dimension. The vibrant paintings on the walls and the canvases in process took the wind from his lungs and breathed life into the room.

"Oh, my God, these are beautiful."

Rebecca's face broke out into a smile. "You really like them?"

His eyes were glued to the mountainside with day lilies and blue and purple flowers dotting the carpet of green grass. The wide sweeping lush forest rose beyond, and a gazebo draped in red roses sat perched on the edge of the mountainside overlooking the valley. "That's the most exquisite place I've ever seen."

"It's my grandmother's house."

"Where Alison and Brady got married?"

"Yes." Rebecca turned to him. "I hope it's not too painful for you."

It took him a minute for the implication to sink in. Did she think he still harbored feelings for her cousin? "I'm happy for Alison," he said truthfully. "I realized that we were just good friends."

"Oh."

"And I meant that the painting is beautiful, Rebecca. I'm not much of an art expert, but any fool can see you captured the essence of the mood of the place in its natural state." His gaze swept the other canvases, the tulip garden, the rock walkway surrounding it, another raw piece of an old clapboard house with an ancient well. "You're very talented."

She fidgeted with a paintbrush on the easel next to her. "I enjoy it."

He met her gaze. "It shows." Every line, every

stroke of the brush, her attention to detail all hinted at the inner woman. The vibrant colors and hues radiated warmth, energy and a passion for life, yet he detected an underlying sensitivity steeped with emotion.

His gaze fell to her slender hands, and he imagined her stroking the brush across the canvas, immersed in the mood of the moment. Then an image of her stroking those long nimble fingers across the bare expanse of his chest flashed into his mind, and his heart began to pound.

If she put that much feeling into her art, what would making love to her be like?

Chapter Eight

Thomas tried his best to shake off the thought and dragged his gaze from her paintings to her face. A big mistake. His praise earned a radiant smile. Pink rose-bud lips turned up like the budding petals of a rose opening to the sun, beckoning for his touch. He stared at her mouth for a hungry moment, watched as her gaze fastened onto his lips. His mouth parted involuntarily. The heartbeat of silence between them stretched into an eternity. Her tongue flicked out to wet her lips, and he nearly groaned out loud at the tiny, sultry movement. His body hardened in response. He wanted to taste her. To trace that trembling pulse at the base of her throat where desire sprang to life. To have her whisper his name in that sweet throaty voice and open up to him.

Good heavens, what was he doing?

He'd toasted her as a friend earlier, and that was all he wanted. Friendship and her connection to her father.

"You really should show these," he said, surprised that his voice worked at all when his brain had taken a disastrous detour into lustful fantasies. Like how Rebecca would look lying in his arms beneath the skylight with only moonlight spilling over her body. Like that rosebud ready to bloom with those petals coming alive for him....

Her smile faded slightly, and she folded her arms beneath her breasts. "No. I paint just for myself and my family."

"And friends."

She blushed again. "I've never done that before."

So he was her first.

A quiver of longing snaked through him again, more intense this time. Would he be her first in other ways, too?

Shaken by that thought, he was grateful when the phone rang. She jerked as if surprised, then stepped over to the end table and looked at the caller ID. She let it ring once, twice.

"Aren't you going to answer it?"

She nodded and picked it up. "Hello, Suzanne."

Girls. They'd probably talk forever. He pounced on the opportunity and decided to leave before he did anything stupid.

But they had had such a nice evening, he didn't want to be rude. So he moved closer to her, then lifted a strand of her silky hair from her neck and whispered, "Thanks for having dinner with me. I had a great time. I'll call you tomorrow." Then without analyzing why or what he was doing, he brushed a gentle kiss to the hollow of her throat.

AT THE FEEL OF THOMAS'S lips on her neck, Rebecca quivered with longing that arose from somewhere deep inside her. Then he disappeared, and she sank onto the couch, breathless, wondering why he'd kissed her. And wishing he hadn't left.

Had she misinterpreted the look he'd given her earlier? She'd thought she'd seen hunger in his eyes. For her.

No, it couldn't be.

He'd said they were friends.

"Rebecca, are you listening?" Suzanne's voice broke into the haze around her.

Still, she savored the sensations spiraling through her, memorizing his masculine scent and the lingering whisper of his kiss. "Yes."

"Are you all right?"

"Yes, I'm fine." *Attracted to a man who is all wrong for me. I want to ask him to give me a baby but I don't have the nerve.*

"Like I was saying, Mimi called earlier, and she and Hannah plan to come to Atlanta on a shopping spree to pick new outfits for the party. I hope you're coming with them."

A shopping trip with all the girls? "I...I don't know."

"Oh, come on, Rebecca, don't be a fuddy-dud. You can use a new wardrobe."

She glanced down at her loose-fitting dress. "What's wrong with my clothes?"

Suzanne sighed. "Nothing, if you want people to think you're an old school marm."

"My clothes are comfortable. Besides, I sell books in a small town—"

"That doesn't mean you have to look like the spinster librarian. Come on, it'll be fun." Suzanne's voice grew excited. "We'll get free makeovers and have lunch. Oh, and there's a great lingerie shop we can buy some fancy underthings, too. You never know when you might be taking your clothes off for some sexy guy!"

Rebecca faked a laugh. Yeah, right. If only she had that problem to worry about.

THOMAS TURNED ON his treadmill and began to walk, then jog, hoping the exercise would purge the desire to call Rebecca and hear her voice again. That stupid kiss had done something to him. His lips had never tasted skin that actually made him tingle from the inside out.

He had wanted to dip his mouth and taste her lips, then lower down her neck and beyond....

He adjusted the speed on the machine and sped up until he was sweating. What was wrong with him?

He'd never been interested in art before, but the passion in those pictures had aroused him and his curiosity about the woman who had painted them. They were just landscapes, for God's sake. It wasn't as if she'd painted nudes or erotic love scenes.

Don't think about the paintings—think about that homey little apartment. All those antiques and family photos and hand-knitted afghans. Rebecca was a homebody. She'd obviously settled in Sugar Hill for life.

And he didn't intend to.

He planned to move on. When he went to Atlanta, he'd find some sophisticated city woman to keep him company. And if he ever did decide to open up his heart again, it would be with someone who enjoyed the same activities he did, hiking and skiing and...and football!

Someone who'd help him in his drive for success.

He picked up the pace and ran until he thought he would collapse. Until the images of Rebecca lying naked beneath that skylight faded and reality returned. Images of Rebecca crashing his car and nearly killing him with her driving replaced the fantasies.

If he allowed himself to care about her, she might break his heart. Or he'd hurt her and feel like a heel when he moved to Atlanta.

His phone jangled, and he turned off the treadmill, swiped a towel across his sweating face and reached for it, half hoping to hear Rebecca's voice on the other end of the line.

Instead Rachel Lackey's frantic husband bellowed with worry. "Rachel's in labor, Doc. And I think—" his voice broke "—I think something's wrong."

REBECCA WAS CERTAIN she wouldn't need new underwear, but she could hardly turn down an outing with her cousins and sister without seeming like a real bore, so she agreed to join them and hung up. She touched her finger to her neck, where her skin felt hot from Thomas's lips. It couldn't hurt to spruce up herself and her wardrobe. Maybe then she could summon up the confidence to ask Thomas about her plan.

Except after that near-kiss, maybe she'd forget about in vitro and consider approaching the baby plan the old-fashioned way. Would she ever have the nerve to ask Thomas? Would he be interested even if she did?

Her gaze landed on the hope chest. She traced a

finger over the intricate carvings on the silver handle of the comb and mirror set, then raised the mirror and looked into the antique glass. What had Thomas thought when he'd looked at her earlier? Did he see a dowdy-looking spinster or the lonely girl who ached inside for love? For a man's touch?

As she placed the mirror in the hope chest, she dragged the handmade afghan over her, then picked up the book of erotic poetry and stretched out on her bed. Several passages later the images the words evoked sprang to life. Bodies entwined. Lovers' lips meeting and parting. Tasting. Exploring. Taunting. Seeking.

She picked up her sketchbook, knowing she had to express herself the only way she knew how. Though she had always blushed and been nervous when she'd had to sketch nudes in her drawing classes, here in the privacy of her bedroom, the lines and angles of the man's body flew from her fingertips. The mouth, the eyes, the subtle hint of a smile, of desire. Broad shoulders, muscles defined, a wide chest narrowing to lean muscular hips. Thick dark hair sprinkled over hard muscular thighs and calves. She hesitated. Told herself not to continue. To tear up the sketch and throw it away, just as she should throw away these silly fantasies.

But her hand disobeyed, and the artist in her continued to sketch, to fill in the details of his physique. Strong. Defined. Bold.

And when she finished, she stared at the face of the man she'd sketched and couldn't believe her eyes. It might have been the best freehand drawing she'd ever done.

Only, no one would ever see it. Especially her subject.

Thomas.

She chuckled sardonically. When she'd been drawing, she hadn't thought once about her baby plan....

IT WAS EARLY MORNING before Thomas allowed himself to leave the hospital. Even then he hated to abandon the Lackeys. The delivery had not gone well, although they had stabilized the baby enough to transfer it to the neonatal unit in Atlanta. He and the pediatrician in town, Josh Redgrave, had both picked up on heart problems. The infant needed surgery right away along with more extensive tests they weren't equipped to conduct at Sugar Hill General.

The Lackeys' reaction had been difficult to handle, the situation frightening for everyone, and Rachel's husband had needed someone to blame. He'd taken his distress out on his wife and Thomas.

He'd bluntly accused Thomas of not giving her proper prenatal care.

Thomas had reviewed the details of Rachel's pregnancy a dozen times, but his answer always went back to the genetics factor, which wasn't the explanation Larry Lackey had wanted to hear. Thomas understood the problems, the anger, the denial, the inclination to blame someone, although there was nothing any of them could have done to predict the infant's health problems. And unfortunately, they still couldn't assure the couple the baby would survive.

The memory of his lovely evening with Rebecca emerged like sunshine breaking through thunderclouds, but he suppressed it immediately as he pulled off his clothes and stretched out on his bed, exhausted. The empty house echoed with silence, the scent of furniture polish and pine cleaner strong. No homey smells like freshly baked brownies or that apple-cinnamony scent he'd detected at Rebecca's.

Forget Rebecca. This house was what he wanted. Big, impressive, perfectly decorated. The kind of place he could entertain a hospital board, even throw a party for potential charity drives. Still, the massive rooms weren't as comforting in the dark of night as he'd imagined when he'd first purchased the house. He closed his eyes and tried to find the peace he so craved, but instead he saw the pale Lackey baby squirming in the incubator and his forlorn parents watching helplessly.

Just like his parents had years ago with his baby brother. And just as he had....

He fisted his hands and pounded the covers. No matter how hard he tried and how much he learned, there would always be problem deliveries, sick infants...

The sooner he moved to Atlanta the better.

"YOU LOOK FABULOUS!" Suzanne shrieked as Mimi modeled a black crepe off-the-shoulder dress that hugged her curves. "And the sapphire blue is you, Hannah."

Mimi giggled and wiggled her hips. "It's nice to have some shape again."

Hannah waved a hand. "Oh, hush, Mimi, you looked fabulous pregnant."

"Yes, you did, Mimi," Rebecca added, imagining her own body growing with a child.

Suzanne held up an emerald-green backless dress. It was slinky and sexy, as if the designer had Suzanne in mind when she'd created it. "What do you think?"

"Try it on," Mimi coached.

"You'll look great in it," Rebecca said. "Of course, with your figure you'd look great in anything."

Suzanne laughed. "Right. With the help of a Wonderbra," Suzanne said. "But it's not so much fun when the clothes come off and the guy realizes half the up-front is not real."

Rebecca shook her head. "I can't imagine any guy being disappointed in you."

"Then tell me why Nick dumped me."

"'Cause he's a fool," Mimi said.

"An idiot," Hannah chimed in.

Suzanne laughed again. "Thanks. I needed that. I've been so depressed about the whole thing. I just can't seem to find anyone serious. Every guy I date in Atlanta just wants sex, no commitments. Is that what I look like? The love-'em-and-leave-'em type?"

"Of course not," Mimi said.

"That's their problem," Hannah said.

"Except it's starting to get to me," Suzanne said, sounding frustrated.

Rebecca quirked her head sideways, surprised at the sincerity in Suzanne's admission. She never thought Suzanne got depressed. Or that any man dumped her.

Whereas, Rebecca's middle name was dump. In high school, three guys had cozied up to her, pretending interest, only to discover they really wanted Suzanne. Memories of prom night her senior year surfaced. When Suzanne's date had come down with the flu the day before the prom, Rebecca's date had canceled right in front of everyone in the lunch line at school, then turned and asked Suzanne in class that afternoon. Of course, Suzanne had refused him. She'd also ditched the other guys when she'd discovered their sneaky plan. But Rebecca had been so humiliated.

The memories resurrected all her old insecurities. She suddenly wanted to go home, to forget this silly shopping trip. To bury herself back in her baggy dresses and books and art.

Oblivious to her thoughts, Suzanne pointed to a rack of custom designed gowns. "Rebecca, get busy and try on some dresses. We still have to check out the lingerie."

Rebecca wrinkled her nose. "I'm not sure any of these are me." They were too expensive. Too showy. Too revealing.

"Are you kidding?" Mimi plucked up a hot-pink dress with spaghetti straps. "Try this one for starters."

"Oh, and you have to try this maroon cocktail dress," Hannah said. "This color will drive men wild."

"And I like this violet off-the-shoulder sheath for you," Suzanne said. "The color will accentuate the blue in your eyes."

"She's right. Play up your best features." Mimi leaned back and gave Rebecca a critical look. "Your eyes are definitely one of them. But you have great curves, too. You simply need to show them off."

"I know. Can you believe it?" Suzanne hitched out a hip. "In middle school, she had great boobs when I was stick straight. All the boys used to swoon over her.''

''They didn't swoon. They gaped and whispered all kinds of moronic cracks,'' Rebecca said in horror. ''I hated it.''

''Well, enjoy it now.'' Mimi pushed her toward the dressing room. ''With your body and sweet personality, you'll be a great catch for some lucky guy.''

''Maybe even a doctor,'' Hannah said.

Rebecca's face felt hot. Had Hannah and Mimi guessed that she was attracted to Thomas? Had they told him?

Mortified at the thought, she gathered the dresses and hurried into the fitting room. Seconds later she teetered out wearing the violet dress along with a pair of sparkly gold heels Mimi had unearthed earlier at a sale rack and convinced her she *had* to have. The criss-cross of the back revealed a lot of skin without being too risqué, and the length fell nicely just below her knees. But the clingy fabric hugged every curvy inch of her. She felt half-naked, as if every fatal flaw she had was flashing like a cheap neon sign.

''You look fantastic,'' Hannah said.

Suzanne whistled. ''No doubt. You have to buy that one.''

''Those have-sex-with-me shoes will snare any man,'' Mimi said. ''Mark my words.''

Rebecca checked the price tag on the dress. ''I don't know—''

Suzanne held up a warning hand. ''Don't argue, sis. I'll pay for it. Consider it an early birthday gift.''

''He'll probably want to take off the dress and just do it with you in the shoes,'' Mimi said.

Rebecca's face blanched.

"Mimi," Hannah said with an eye roll, "you're incorrigible."

Mimi batted innocent eyes. "Well, he will."

Suzanne grinned. "She's right. And you have to call us and tell us all the juicy details the morning after."

As if there were going to be a romantic rendezvous with juicy details and a morning after. Rebecca ducked back inside the fitting room to change, heat flushing over her entire body.

Three hours later the girls left the shopping mall, each with several packages. Rebecca had a new wardrobe. Suzanne and Mimi and Hannah had dragged her from store to store, selecting casual clothes as well as dating clothes, everything from jeans and sweaters to casual slacks and silk camisoles and T-shirts to party dresses, shoes and lingerie. Then they'd stopped by the cosmetic counter for a quick makeover, then browsed through the bath shop for bubble bath and oils along with scented candles and lotions and body sprays.

Like she *needed* a lot of dating clothes and bubble bath and body sprays!

And the underwear…ohh, her skin tingled just thinking about the soft scraps of decadent lace. She had never felt sexier than when she'd tried on the skimpy pieces, just like Mimi promised.

What would Thomas think of the selections?

She shook her head, unable to believe her own straying thoughts. Thomas would not see her underwear.

"We're going to the baby department," Mimi said.

"I have to find Maggie Rose something to wear to the party, too."

"You're not going to dress Maggie in those pink frilly dresses, like the ones *you* refused to wear, are you, Mimi?" Hannah asked with a wink.

"Well, she's a little young for belly dancing clothes or sequins," Mimi said. "But maybe we can find something in between."

The girls laughed, but Rebecca's heart fluttered. She'd give anything to be picking out her own baby's clothes.

"While they visit the infant department, let's call Dad's office and stop by if he's in," Suzanne suggested. "We can talk to him about Grammy Rose's party."

Rebecca resisted the urge to balk. As much as she dreaded seeing her father dote on Suzanne the entire party, her grandmother would be disappointed if he didn't attend.

But what if he and Uncle Wiley broke out into a fight and ruined the surprise party?

THOMAS HAD A TERRIBLE Saturday. Instead of catching up on the latest medical journals, which he usually did on his day off, he couldn't concentrate for worrying about the Lackey baby. He'd phoned the Atlanta hospital only to be put off twice. The doctors had been running tests, concurring, administering more tests. Then they'd had to meet with the Lackeys.

The diagnosis included extensive surgery involving the baby's heart and lungs. He would stay in the hospital for weeks. And still there was the off chance that he might not survive.

Thomas reviewed every sonogram he'd taken during Rachel's pregnancy, looking for any details that might have clued him in to a problem, but found nothing. The realization that he couldn't have detected the boy's health problems alleviated some of his anxiety but also made him feel weak and powerless, limited by mankind and technology. He needed more expertise, more cutting-edge technology.

He paced the confines of his office when a knock jerked his head up. Otis Sandler had phoned him first thing this morning. He'd pulled together a work crew of teenagers to paint the exam rooms and would complete the project sooner than Thomas anticipated.

"We've finished the first three rooms," Otis said. "We can get the others done tomorrow."

"You don't have to work on Sunday," Thomas said.

Otis shrugged. "The boys want to. They're all trying to earn money for their senior trip."

Thomas shrugged. "All right."

As soon as the crew left, the place felt empty and quiet. Just like his big house would, which was the reason he'd had to leave this morning. His own doubts and fears had echoed off the ten-foot ceilings all night.

Frustrated but not knowing where he intended to go, he grabbed his keys and headed to the yellow Mustang. His Porsche should be ready in a few days, he'd have to tell Rebecca so she could stop worrying.

Rebecca. He'd tried not to think about her today. About how her neck had tasted. About that artwork and the passion he sensed within the quiet, shy girl who'd painted it.

He zipped out of the parking lot, telling himself he

would not go to see Rebecca. Not tonight. Not when he felt needy and lonely.

But he ended up at her apartment anyway. Knocking on the door. Wondering what he'd say if she answered.

Wondering what he'd do if she didn't.

Chapter Nine

Rebecca felt decadent. After leaving her sister in Atlanta and listening to Hannah and Mimi chatter on about how their hope chests had triggered the events that had resulted in their proposals, her imagination had gone wild. Maybe there was something to the magic surrounding the hope chests, after all.

Optimistic, she'd spread all her new purchases across her bed and imagined wearing them for Thomas. Finally she decided to experiment with the bath products and aromatherapy candles. The combination of lavender, ylang-ylang and grapefruit was supposed to relax her. The lavender candle represented comfort in romance, idealism and tranquility. Mimi claimed cinnamon was supposed to be especially enticing to a man.

Did the apple-cinnamon muffins she'd baked for the meals on wheels count? She could smell them in the house.

Not that she had any exciting plans later....

No, if she did, she'd use the jasmine perfume that had cost way too much. Just a little dab at the nape of the neck and between her breasts promised to drive men wild with desire. Just what she'd like to do with Thomas. Then she could have a good old-fashioned evening of sexy lovemaking…the way a baby was meant to be created.

The thought made her grow still for a moment. Was she acting out of desperation or selfishness to want a child of her own?

In a perfect world, Thomas would fall in love with her, and the question would be moot. She closed her eyes, remembering the erotic poetry Grammy Rose had given her. The words hummed through her head in a sultry melody.

The doorbell rang and she froze, the hot bubbly water sloshing around her as she grappled with the return to reality.

What if it was Jerry?

The mere idea obliterated the poetry from her mind.

She still hadn't talked to him about New Year's Eve, and it was only two nights away. Surely he'd gotten the hint.

The doorbell chimed again.

Drat.

She didn't want a romantic evening or any other kind with the clumsy oaf.

Knowing she couldn't stall the final no forever, she dried off, then pulled on her new velour robe and tied the sash, grinning as she remembered the girls raving about the rose color highlighting the natural rosy glow of her cheeks. She checked the antique mirror from the hope chest—yep, pink as a rose.

Not that she wanted to look especially good or rosy for Jerry. Quite the opposite. She didn't want to give him the wrong idea. Maybe she should close those cinnamon muffins up tight before she opened the door, and put on her ratty flannel.

The doorbell blared again. He was awfully persistent tonight.

Steeling herself to whip out a fast refusal to any invitations he might offer, she opened the door. But instead of the big-bellied neighbor with the leering eyes, Thomas stood on the other side.

And his eyes definitely weren't leering. They were sinfully wanting as they traveled over her, all the way from the damp tendrils of her hair down to her bare hot-pink toes. Toes that curled upward at the wild heat flaring in his eyes.

THOMAS HAD NO IDEA why he'd driven to Rebecca's except that her place reminded him of comfort and home, and she was safe.

At least, he'd thought she was safe.

Until she'd opened the door.

Good grief! What had she done to herself? The exotic scents of some kind of body bath floated around him, the scent of cinnamon and lavender and sultry woman colliding in one big sensory storm that assaulted his nerve endings and took his arousal to a completely new level.

"Thomas?" her voice squeaked out, hoarse and throaty which only cranked that arousal up another notch.

"I...I..." Why had he come? "I wanted to tell you that the painters came today." Lame. Lame. Lame. "So you can start the murals anytime." *Now go, before you peel off that puff of a robe and taste that delicious skin.*

''Oh?'' She fidgeted with the top of her robe. If she was trying to cover herself, it was too damn late. He'd already spied more than a hint of cleavage and realized that Rebecca had indeed been hiding some very nice curves. Some very voluptuous curves that jumpstarted all kinds of wicked fantasies.

''That was fast.''

He nodded mutely. What were they talking about?

''D-did you want to come in?''

Did he? Lord, yes.

Should he? Hell, no.

''Thomas, are you all right?''

''It's been a bad day.''

''Oh, I'm sorry.'' Her voice dripped with sweet concern. ''Come on in. I can make some coffee or tea.''

''C-coffee would be great.'' Now *he* was stuttering. But as she turned and he followed her to the small kitchen alcove, he was so mesmerized by the sway of her hips encased in that slinky rose material, he forgot to speak altogether. Some men preferred skinny women like the thin models in magazines, but he definitely preferred a woman with shape.

And Rebecca had plenty of curves.

Hands jammed into his pockets so he wouldn't touch her, he watched as she busied herself starting coffee. She also turned on the teapot and removed two cups from the oak cupboard, then sat sweetener in a small dish on the bar and poured milk into a dainty little creamer with tulips painted on the side. Finally she offered him a cinnamon muffin. ''I make them for the meals on wheels,'' she explained.

That comment should have yanked his libido back in place fast, but he was too far gone.

"So, what happened today, Thomas?"

His frustration and worry over the boy's future returned.

The way Larry Lackey had blamed him.

His desire for anything but comfort forgotten, he told her about the delivery.

REBECCA HAD NEVER SEEN anyone look so miserable as he relayed the excruciating details of the difficult delivery and Larry Lackey's accusations. In light of the guilt Lackey's words evoked, the weight and responsibility of Thomas's job seemed even more magnified.

She could no more resist comforting him than she could resist drawing her next breath. She took the stool beside him and pressed her hand over his. "Mr. Lackey was just in pain, Thomas," Rebecca said softly. "Lashing out, reacting out of anger. I'm sure he didn't mean what he said. He'll realize it and apologize later."

"I know that, but still, if there was more I could have done..." Thomas stretched his fingers out in front of him as if he had to examine his hands for any flaws. "I've reviewed all Rachel Lackey's files—"

"And there was no way you could have predicted the child's problem." She squeezed his hand, feeling the tension knotted in his fingers as he gripped hers tightly. "You're not God, Thomas. You're a doctor. You can only do the best you can, and then put it in *His* hands."

He stared at her as if she was speaking some foreign language, but somewhere deep in those green eyes she saw the struggle. He wanted to believe her, yet the

Lackeys' attitude and his own baby brother's death haunted him.

''It's not that I'm a religious fanatic, but I do believe in faith,'' Rebecca continued softly. ''You have a talent, Thomas, and you're using it. That's a blessing.'' She felt more tension draining slowly from him as his hand relaxed into hers. ''Do the Lackeys realize how lucky they were that they have you as their doctor? Just think what might have happened if you *hadn't* been there.'' Her voice gained momentum. ''What if we didn't have an OB-GYN in Sugar Hill, or what if we had some old geezer who didn't keep up with the latest advances in medicine? Someone who didn't care? Then where would the town be?''

''I never thought about it like that.''

''Then think about it now.'' Anger simmered below the surface of her words. ''Hannah's a great family practitioner, but she's not a specialist, Thomas. Sugar Hill needs you.''

His gaze dropped to their joined hands for a long moment that was fraught with tension. The ticking of the antique cuckoo clock in the background amplified the silence while the whisper of his breath awakened instincts long dormant.

Then he shocked her by lifting her hand to his mouth and pressing his lips to the tender surface.

Rebecca's breath caught in her chest.

''You are such a sweetheart,'' Thomas said. ''I've never met anyone like you, Rebecca.'' He closed his eyes and brought their joined hands up to his cheek, then leaned against them.

Rebecca ached for him. She forgot her shyness.

Her inhibitions. That this man was a part of some baby plan.

She simply wanted to hold him.

With a strangled sigh of his name, she gently touched his cheek, then angled his face until he looked into her eyes. Their gazes locked for a tender moment, then the anguish in his expression melted away and something hot and primal replaced it.

He caught her face between his hands, lowered his mouth and kissed her.

THOMAS HAD NO IDEA what overcame him, except that possessing Rebecca, even in some small way, drove him like a demon. She was the nicest, most honest, most compassionate woman he'd ever known. She volunteered at the church, organized a reading club to encourage kids, and her quiet compassion allowed him to voice his most troubled thoughts.

He'd never tasted lips so sweet and gentle, or touched a woman's cheek that aroused him the way her soap-scented tender skin did.

He deepened the kiss, teasing her lips apart with his tongue until he dove inside to explore the recesses of her mouth, just as he wanted to explore her mind.

And her heart.

Beneath that lovely figure beat the heart of an angel.

And the womanly body of a temptress.

His hand trailed slowly down to trace a path along her jaw, grazed across the slender column of her neck, stroked the curve of her shoulder until he pulled her against him. He felt the small tremors in her body as her breasts pushed into his chest. His heart racing, he tore his mouth from hers to nibble at her ear, then lower to the sensitive shell of her ear. And when he dipped below to her neck and tasted the lavender there, she moaned softly and clung to his arms. His other hand snaked into her hair and tugged at the gold clasp binding it, and he dropped the clasp to the counter with a clatter. Her nails dug into his arms as he threaded his fingers into the tangled tresses and combed them down over her shoulders. He pushed the robe gently aside so long, blond hair spilled onto bare shoulders.

Then he pulled back to look at her. Her cheeks were flushed, her vibrant eyes alight with passion. The low moan that erupted from her parted lips nearly tore him in two. The provocative hint of the forbidden shimmered in the slight tremble of her body as his gaze devoured the tantalizing sight of her bare shoulders.

He wanted more.

Wanted to lower that robe and taste the innocent erotic flesh below. To strip her of everything and then let his skin slide across hers in a sinful game of torture.

He had never felt this way about a woman before.

The power of the emotion shook him to the core.

''Thomas.'' She murmured his name so softly it shouldn't have stirred his sex but it did, as if his body had its own mind and that mind longed to be joined with hers.

But he couldn't take her here.

Not out of some selfish need, when she'd only meant to offer him comfort.

The phone rang, saving him from speaking. She frowned and glanced at it as if she didn't know whether to answer it or not. He didn't want her to. He wanted to continue their lovemaking.

But he forced himself to be a gentleman. ''Go ahead and get it.''

She took another long hard look at him, the passionate glaze in her eyes still burning, then slowly pulled her robe back over her shoulders and picked up the phone.

''Hello, Suzanne.''

Her sister had saved him once again.

''You talked to Dad?'' She paused and tucked a strand of that silky hair behind her ear. ''He's coming tomorrow?''

Thomas picked up the coffee and sipped it though it had gotten cold, the strong brew calmed him and dragged him back to his senses.

She wound the phone cord around her fingers. ''Okay, I'll see you both at the coffee shop at noon.''

She hung up, gnawing on her lower lip.

''Something wrong?''

''N-no, my father's coming to town with Suzanne tomorrow. We're going to t-talk to him about Grammy's party.''

She was stuttering again. He wasn't sure what that meant. Had she realized how far they'd almost gone and regretted it?

''I'm sorry if I overstepped, Rebecca.'' He backed away, afraid if he touched her again, he'd start all over. And this time he wouldn't be able to stop. The force of his need stunned him.

She folded her arms across her chest. ''I…you don't have to apologize.''

''I'd better go.''

She simply watched him, then nodded. But when

she walked him to the door, he sensed she wanted to say more.

It didn't matter. He could not seduce her, then ask her father for a job. What kind of man would that make him?

"I-if you want to give me a key, I can do the painting at night," she said, filling the awkward silence.

He nodded this time. "Hannah and I will work it out."

Her eyebrow rose at that, but he decided it might be better if Hannah dealt with her and the paintings. Just look how her art and the tantalizing scents in her apartment affected him now.

He grabbed his keys from his pocket and jangled them in his hand. "Thanks for letting me unload on you, Rebecca."

"Anytime." A small smile curved her mouth. "And I meant what I said. Sugar Hill is lucky to have you."

That comment sparked a second of guilt for deceiving her, for allowing her to think he was committed to staying here to practice. Still his gaze caught a glimpse of the whisker burn on her neck, and he knew he had to leave. Fast.

In fact, maybe he'd stop by the café tomorrow around lunchtime. Then he could meet her father and he wouldn't have to swing an invitation to that family party.

Yes, that was a better plan.

Then he wouldn't have to see Rebecca again.

Or be tempted to take her to bed, when he knew he would soon be gone.

REBECCA CLOSED THE DOOR and locked the dead bolt, her head spinning. What had just happened between her and Thomas?

One minute she'd been offering him comfort, the next minute he'd kissed her hungrily. She touched her finger to her lips, the sizzle of his touch still tormenting her. She had never experienced anything as sensual as Thomas's hot mouth on hers.

And, Lord help her, she wanted to experience it again. And much more.

So why had he pulled away?

Had she come across as inexperienced? She'd thought they were perfect....

Had he realized that he was holding shy, awkward Rebecca Hartwell in his arms and decided he wanted something else? Something more?

Frustration gnawed at her. She'd actually sensed they shared an emotional connection earlier, had thought those emotions had triggered his desire for her. Could she have been wrong? Had he needed comfort so badly he would have sought it from whomever was available?

Confused, she paced the den, then reheated her tea, and forced herself to down it. Thomas had pulled away emotionally, just as her father had so many years ago when her mother had died.

Her father had had no time for anyone but Suzanne. Rebecca didn't understand his reasons. But her father had no longer hugged her or probed her about schoolwork or friends. In fact, when she'd walked into a room, he'd looked at her with such sadness in his eyes that she thought he blamed her for her mother's death.

Then one day he'd finally stopped looking at her at all. It was as if she'd become invisible to him.

She had to see him tomorrow.

Tears welled up in her eyes as the memories bombarded her. So many nights she'd lain in her bed and wondered why her father didn't love her anymore. Had wondered what was wrong with her.

She picked up the antique hand mirror and gazed at her reflection, frowning as her troubled expression stared back. Grammy's words echoed in her head. *Believe in yourself. Follow your dream.*

Thomas's words chimed afterward. *You are the sweetest thing. I've never met anyone like you.*

Suzanne and her cousins had assured her today she was beautiful.

So, why couldn't Thomas love her?

Chapter Ten

Thomas hurried toward the bookstore, determined not to miss Bert Hartwell. He would meet the man today, get a feel for his personality and be better prepared for the interview he'd already scheduled.

Then he would avoid Rebecca.

No more dropping by her apartment late at night. No more mindboggling kisses or tantalizing touches that left him achy. No more seeking comfort from her when he knew he'd be leaving town soon. She might have claimed she didn't want marriage, but he couldn't fathom a nice girl like her settling for anything less.

And he didn't intend on marrying and settling down in this sleepy little town.

Mary Anne Turner waved to him from across the square, and he offered her a friendly wave back. But he saw Benita in front of the drugstore and Karina Peterson exiting the bridal shop with a bridal magazine in her hands and he picked up his pace. Pretending he didn't see them, he ducked inside the Hot Spot entrance, planning to use lunch and coffee as his excuse.

He saw Rebecca the minute he entered, and his heart tripped in his chest.

She'd exchanged the loose-fitting dresses she normally wore for a tailored suit in dark blue that hugged her figure. Instead of touching her ankles, this skirt rode just above her knees, offering him a tantalizing view of shapely calves. Her hair seemed blonder, her legs longer, her eyes even more blue. And those pink lips even more kissable.

Annoyed at his reaction, he barely managed to pull himself together before she glanced from the table where she stood and caught his eye. A small spark of surprise lit the depths, then her mouth curved in a smile. Before he could speak to her, a blustery man in an expensive suit with balding hair and a short beard approached her, his hand placed on Suzanne's arm, which was tucked inside his. The man must be her father, Bert. He walked with a worldly, sophisticated air that started with the tilt of his chin and scrutinizing gaze and was magnified by his conservative, expensive suit. He was the complete opposite of Wiley Hartwell, in his bright lime-green suits. Now he understood why these men might have problems.

Thomas joined the end of the sandwich line, listening to the Hartwells with one ear while he ordered.

"Hi, Rebecca." Bert barely glanced at her as he pulled out the chair beside him for Suzanne. Rebecca moved to the opposite side, fidgeting with her hands as she grabbed a menu.

His heart gave a funny tug. Thomas was tempted to take her hands in his and still them, but he held himself in check. He couldn't interfere with the dynamics of a family he didn't know, much less understand.

Suzanne dominated the conversation, chatting to fill the air while Rebecca melted deeper into her chair.

Bert laughed and patted Suzanne's hand, doting on her every word.

Why was Rebecca so uncomfortable around her father? And why did he seem to be ignoring her?

"Thomas, what would you like today?" Mimi's bright, cheery smile flashed from behind the counter.

"Oh...the chicken sandwich, I guess. And coffee."

"Comin' right up," Mimi chirped.

He forced a smile, wondering if he should approach the threesome or find his own table. Although the café was packed, a couple of tables in the far corner remained vacant, but sitting in the rear would make it difficult to catch Bert if he decided to leave abruptly.

He paid for his food and accepted it from Mimi.

"Come on, Thomas, I want you to meet someone," Mimi said.

Thomas squinted at her as she sauntered from behind the counter and dragged him over to Rebecca's table. "Uncle Bert, hey!" Mimi hugged her uncle. "There's someone I want you to meet. Our town OB-GYN, Dr. Thomas Emerson. He works with Hannah."

Rebecca and Suzanne both looked up in surprise while Bert stood and pumped his hand. "Nice to meet you, son. Bert Hartwell. Why don't you join us?"

Thomas glanced at Rebecca to gauge her reaction but he couldn't read it. He vowed to thank Mimi if he wound up landing the job in Atlanta.

MIMI GRABBED HANNAH as soon as she entered the café and hauled her to the corner. "Uncle Bert's over there with Suzanne and Rebecca and Thomas."

"Thomas?"

''Yes,'' Mimi said, preening like a proud peacock. ''You should have seen him. He couldn't take his eyes off Rebecca.''

''Really?'' Hannah shot a look their way. ''He hasn't said anything.''

''Just give them some time. Maybe if we keep pushing them together, something will happen.''

''I hope so,'' Hannah said. ''Because this matchmaking scheme of yours could blow up in your face, and that might mean disaster for Rebecca.''

''That's so not going to happen,'' Mimi boasted. ''They're meant to be together.''

Hannah rolled her eyes. ''Come on, I promised Suzanne we'd provide backup in case Uncle Bert balks at the idea of the party.''

''What are we supposed to say about Dad?''

Hannah motioned for Mimi to follow. ''This time, you follow my lead.''

REBECCA GAVE THOMAS a quick hello, then toyed with her coffee stirrer. His arm brushed hers as he sat down, and she remembered the feel of his hands and mouth on her body the night before. Heat spread up her neck at the sensations the memory triggered.

Why had Mimi dragged him over here? She knew they were having a family meeting to talk their father into attending the party. A busy doctor like Thomas certainly wouldn't be interested in their family problems, especially brotherly bickering.

Mimi and Hannah approached and claimed seats on the end.

''Now, what's this little meeting all about?'' Bert

asked. "I know you didn't drag me all the way to Sugar Hill for nothing, Suz."

"You're right, Dad." Suzanne laughed lightly. "We're planning a surprise party for Grammy's seventy-fifth birthday and you have to be there. The whole family is coming."

Bert cleared his throat, thick graying eyebrows narrowing. "You know I'm not comfortable with these big family affairs. I'll send a nice gift."

"No," Hannah said. "You need to come to the party."

Mimi batted her incredibly long lashes. "You're Grammy's oldest son, Uncle Bert, she'll be disappointed if you don't attend."

"We've made all the arrangements," Hannah added. "All you have to do is show up."

"And bring that present yourself," Suzanne said, eliciting a round of laughter.

Thomas dug into his sandwich, and Rebecca flashed him another smile. He must be bored out of his mind.

Bert pulled at his tie, frowning. "What about Wiley? Will he be there, too?"

"Of course," Mimi said. "Dad wouldn't miss it for the world."

"And he knows I'm coming?" Bert glanced at Thomas. "My brother and I don't always see eye to eye."

"Yes, Dad wants you there," Hannah said.

"Right." Bert huffed. "Probably thought I wouldn't show up and he'd get to be the good son."

Rebecca frowned. "Showing Grammy you and Uncle Wiley can get along will be the best surprise you can give her, Dad."

"She's right," Hannah said.

Bert shrugged but still looked skeptical. "I suppose I should come."

"Great. We'll count on it." Mimi hopped up. "Now I have to get back to work."

"Me, too," Hannah said. Mimi and Hannah both hugged Rebecca's father goodbye and left, talking in hushed voices.

"So, young man," Bert said, diverting the conversation toward Thomas. "Tell me about your practice here in Sugar Hill."

Rebecca watched silently as the two men delved into a discussion of the clinic and other details of their medical practices. Thomas reminded her of her father in so many ways, his intellect, his vocation, even his work schedule.

"Graduated from Emory University, huh?" Bert asked, sipping his coffee.

"Yes, sir. I finished a residency at Harvard a couple of years ago."

"Did you hear that, Suzanne?" Bert curved an arm around her shoulders. "This guy is on the ball."

"I know, Dad," Suzanne said, grinning. "Quite impressive."

"Suzanne's on the move herself," Bert bragged. "She attended Georgia State and works in one of the largest land development firms in Atlanta. She's really going places."

Rebecca edged back more in her seat. She was content with her job, so why did her father's constant praise of her sister make her feel as if she was a failure in his eyes?

FOR THE NEXT TWENTY MINUTES, Thomas listened to Bert sing Suzanne's praises, both professionally and personally. Not only was she successful, but when Bert was between wives, she played hostess to his fund-raisers and hospital benefits.

Not once did he mention Rebecca. Why?

Even more disturbing, Rebecca shrank deeper into the wooden chair, becoming more and more invisible as the conversation progressed.

His irritation mounted when Bert practically suggested that he and Suzanne should get together.

''Did Rebecca tell you we've commissioned her to do some artwork for the clinic?'' Thomas asked, changing the subject. He had no intention of dating Suzanne after kissing Rebecca. But he didn't want to turn off Bert Hartwell, either.

Maybe this premeeting hadn't been such a good idea.

''No,'' Bert said. ''Is she donating a painting to the clinic?''

''No, she's designing murals for all the exam rooms. But she should be showing her artwork. I bet the galleries in Atlanta would love to feature her work.''

Rebecca nearly choked on her coffee. ''I...don't think so.''

''She's very talented.'' Thomas reached out and stroked her arm. ''But I'm sure you're already aware of her artistic abilities.''

Bert shifted so the wooden chair squeaked beneath him. ''Well, yes, of course.'' Frowning, he checked his watch and pushed his chair back. ''Look at the time. I really have to be going. I have a board meeting this afternoon. Full schedule...you know how that is, Dr. Emerson."

"Certainly. It was a pleasure to meet you."

Bert stood and draped his arm around Suzanne. "Ready, honey?"

"Sure, Dad. Whenever you are."

Bert shook Thomas's hand. "Maybe we could talk some more later." He scratched his chin. "Hey, why don't you come to the party next week? It'll be nice to have a colleague there. Be a good buffer between me and my brother."

Thomas fought a frown. Bert had extended an invitation to get to know him better, yet he'd shrugged off Rebecca's talent as if it were unimportant. Still, he couldn't refuse Bert's offer. "Thank you, sir. I'd be honored to be your guest."

Did Bert have another agenda in mind? Like pushing his youngest daughter toward him again? And why had he totally neglected the praise he should have given Rebecca?

Rebecca caught him before he left. "Thomas, that was really polite of you to accept my dad's invitation, but you don't have to attend the party. It'll just be a boring family affair."

Guilt mushroomed in his stomach. "That's okay, I don't mind. That is, unless you don't want me to go."

"Oh, no, it's not that." She gestured awkwardly with her hands. "But I don't want you to feel indebted."

He shook his head. "Don't worry about it, Rebecca. I'm looking forward to the party. It's always nice to network with other professionals."

He hurried out the door then, before he revealed his

true motive. But oddly he realized he'd meant what he'd told Rebecca—he was looking forward to the party.

Because he'd get to spend more time with her.

LATER THAT AFTERNOON, just before Rebecca left work, Suzanne phoned.

"Uh-oh, there isn't a problem with Dad, is there?" Rebecca asked. "Did he change his mind about Grammy's party?"

"No. Of course, he mouthed off about Uncle Wiley all the way to Atlanta, but he promised not to back out.... So, sis, tell me what's going on between you and that hunky doctor."

Rebecca sighed and closed her eyes, willing it to be more than her imagination. "Nothing."

"Nothing?" Suzanne's laughter erupted. "You're kidding. That guy is totally hot for you."

"What?" Rebecca's eyes popped open.

"You mean to tell me you didn't notice? You can't be that blind, Bec."

"You're wrong, Suzanne. Thomas is simply nice to everyone."

"Ha! I'm not wrong. He couldn't keep his eyes off you." Suzanne whistled low. "And the way he bragged about your art, good gracious, I thought he was going to offer to be your agent and sell your work himself."

"He wouldn't do that." No, he was not that enthusiastic. "He was just being nice."

"You are so naive, Bec," Suzanne said. "He was *not* just being nice. Now, what's your plan?"

"Plan?"

"Yeah, has he asked you out yet?"

"No. Well, we had dinner, but that was business."

"Right." Another peal of laughter. "Listen, just play it cool. Lead him on a little. And be sure to wear that sexy new underwear. If you feel sexy, you'll be sexier."

Rebecca shook her head and hung up a minute later, certain Suzanne was mistaken. Thomas was not enamored with her. In fact, as soon as everyone else had left, he'd run off, too.

Still, his compliments had boosted her ego. Maybe she'd drop by and start that art project tonight. Maybe she'd even go early and run into him.

She rummaged through her lingerie drawer—where had she put those black lace panties?

THOMAS LEFT THE CLINIC as early as possible. He wanted to check on the Lackey baby in person, so he'd driven to Atlanta and met with the doctors.

Hell, who was he kidding? He had wanted to avoid running into Rebecca.

Dammit, he'd acted like a fool today at lunch. Jumping to her defense, bragging about her artwork, looking at her all goo-goo-eyed. What had happened to him?

One minute Bert had been pushing Suzanne toward him, the next Thomas had lost his tongue and gushed about her sister. But his temper had flared with Bert....

That emotional outburst disturbed him the most. Why the hell should he care about Bert's relationship with his daughters or how much praise the man gave Rebecca?

Because he was beginning to care for her himself.

No, he couldn't....

Frustrated, he left the Atlanta hospital, veered onto the expressway and wound through the traffic until he reached the new women's center in the heart of Buckhead. It was almost New Year's Eve and, barring emergency deliveries, he had the next four days off. He'd signed up for a seminar on fertility treatments at Emory University and would be in Atlanta the next two days. He'd return to Sugar Hill for New Year's Eve.

He parked the car and stared up at the multidimensional complex, at the modern structure and the assorted attached buildings. The architecture was as modern and cutting edge as the research and work conducted inside.

He wanted to be a part of the medical community of Atlanta, here in the heart of this fast-growing city with its high-rises and emergency units and the latest equipment and technology.

So unlike the sleepy backward town of Sugar Hill. Except for Rebecca...

No, her clothes, art, everything about her embodied family and tradition, while his job relied on future technology, not sentiment and emotion. In fact, too much emotion could handicap him in an emergency, the very reason he had to remain compassionate but somewhat detached.

No, he couldn't give up his dreams.

Especially for a case of simple lust....

Chapter Eleven

Two local teenagers helped Gertrude with the inventory in the bookstore, giving Rebecca extra time to work on the murals. Hannah had taken a few days off for the holidays and was only accepting emergency calls, but she had opened the clinic each morning. Apparently, Thomas was in Atlanta attending a medical seminar.

That night after she'd seen Thomas at the café with her father, Rebecca had hoped to see him at the clinic. When he hadn't shown up, she'd wondered if he'd been avoiding her. Now, she was almost certain he'd given her the brush-off.

Thomas didn't owe her anything. Just because he'd kissed her once or twice, she couldn't let it go to her head.

She finished the last touches on the jungle scene, stood back and admired the bright colors of the parrots and wild animals, pleased with the way the piece had turned out. The first day, she'd painted a dinosaur diorama. She'd kept it so simple with bold colors and lines, she'd finished it in one day. Tomorrow she would add some color to the foliage in the jungle scene, detail the tiger's stripes and face, and finish the giraffe. If she arrived early, she could complete it by late afternoon, then head to the festivities at her uncle Wiley's used-car lot and the picnic at the park. That is, if the winter storm didn't blow in and cancel the celebration.

If she had nothing better to do later on in the evening, she would return and work some more. Anything to avoid New Year's Eve with her big-bellied neighbor, Jerry Ruthers.

What would Thomas be doing tomorrow night? Was he staying in Atlanta?

Would he be sharing a New Year's Eve kiss with some woman there?

Pushing aside the disturbing thought, she cleaned up her art supplies, then couldn't resist. She'd seen several books on pregnancy and in vitro fertilization and decided to explore them. Drying her hands on a paper towel, she pulled *The Pregnancy Bible* off the shelf, sat down and began to read.

THOMAS WAS EXHILARATED by the pool of knowledge, the innovative techniques and the level of expertise of the other attendees as well as the speakers at the seminar. The plans for cutting-edge research with high-risk deliveries and birth defects was phenomenal, and the genetic engineering and fertility treatments that had only been a pipe dream ten years before were now being explored and implemented.

He hailed a cab to a local lounge to join a few of the other attendees, doctors from all over the country, for drinks and conversation. The smoke-filled bar was packed with the happy-hour crowd, people enjoying time off for holidays and, from the looks of the mix, the singles set. He had forgotten the difficulty of finding a companion in the crowds, and the taxing ordeal of the meat-market scene.

He wove through the throng until he spotted the group of men and women from the seminar and ordered a scotch. Shawnee Blake, a fertility specialist from Savannah, brushed his arm as he moved into the crowded corner. Attractive, with medium-length auburn hair and a nice smile, she started the conversation ball with chitchat. The usual info, Where are you from? What's your specialty? etcetera, drifted into a discussion of small-town medicine versus metropolitan life, and horror stories of a few bungled cases in the rural parts of Georgia that made his skin crawl and cemented his decision not to have a child unless he lived near a modern facility. The discussion finally turned to personal lives. "I've been married twice," Devon Rourke, the young surgeon, stated. "With my schedule, I decided not to go that route again."

"I know what you mean," Rob Wheeler, a cardiologist from Charleston commented. "I've tried a couple of long-term relationships, but sooner or later the women get fed up with my schedule."

"Being single is more fun anyway," Devon commented.

"How about you, Shawnee?" Rob asked.

She shrugged, lifting her drink for a toast. "I've been swamped with my residency and then research." She gave Thomas a sideways grin, hinting at her attraction. "For now I just want to have a good time."

The men clinked their glasses with hers, toasting the single life.

Just what he wanted to hear, too, Thomas thought, as he raised his glass. Wasn't it? And was he attracted to her?

"So, do you have a woman in Sugar Hill?" she asked.

"No one special." Rebecca's face flashed into his mind, then the parade of women with casseroles and desserts. "But there are a lot of husband-hunting women."

"Must be rough," Devon said.

"Yeah, the town's so small I treat almost every woman there." Except for Rebecca, who'd never seen him as a patient.

"I can't imagine knowing my patients that well," Devon said.

"Me, neither," Rob added. "I barely recognize the nurses and remember my receptionist's name."

"They're just faces in the crowd," Shawnee said.

Thomas frowned. They sounded so impersonal and detached from their patients and work. Was that what it would be like to work in a big medical center? Would it make him immune to the personal side of the job and the people he treated?

ON THE WAY TO HER uncle Wiley's, Rebecca passed the bookstore and was surprised to see Gertrude's car still parked behind. Curious as to why the young woman wasn't at the town celebration, she hurried inside and found her dusting the shelves, her curly brown hair in a ponytail.

"Goodness, why are you still working?" Rebecca frowned at the sad look on Gertrude's face.

Gertrude's shoulders fell. "I don't have anything better to do."

Rebecca's heart tugged. Hadn't she felt that way a hundred times this year? She should have made it a point to befriend the woman.

"Come on with me. I'm going by Uncle Wiley's to see who wins that truck. Then we can stop and get a picnic dinner on the square if the weather holds up."

A smile burst onto Gertrude's face and Rebecca jotted a mental note to invite her to do things more often. It wasn't as if her own social calendar was booked solid.

Gertrude brushed off her jeans, her step lighter as she followed Rebecca outside. A gust of wind swirled around them, rustling trees and scattering dust. The air smelled crisp, heavy with the scent of impending rain and storm clouds. If the temperature kept dropping, the rain might turn to snow.

"It's only a few blocks so you can ride with me," Rebecca offered. "I'll drive you back for your car afterward."

Gertrude climbed in and buckled her seat belt. "You think a lot of people will be there?"

"I imagine so. Everyone's talking about Uncle Wiley giving away that pickup truck." Rebecca steered through the downtown and turned toward the used car lot. "And he's filming a commercial. People will probably show up hoping they'll get on TV."

"I put my name in for the giveaway," Gertrude said, picking at her sweater. "But I know I won't win. I'm not very lucky."

"You never know," Rebecca said. "Maybe this is your lucky day." And maybe it would be hers, too.

Maybe Thomas would show up and they'd end up together.

A glum expression clouded Gertrude's eyes. "If that was true, Jerry Ruthers would have asked me out for tonight."

Jerry? She had no idea her helper had a crush on Jerry. "Maybe he'll be there," she said. "Besides, if you want him, you should pursue him."

Wasn't that the same advice her cousins and sister had given her about Thomas?

Gertrude's brown eyes lit up. "You really think so?" She rummaged through her purse for a mirror and grabbed a tube of ruby-red lipstick, applying it carefully, her spirits brightening.

When Rebecca saw Jerry, she would hint that Gertrude liked him. It might be the answer for all of them.

A half hour later, she and Gertrude had watched the miniparade of old model cars her uncle had arranged, laughed at the children having their faces painted and the residents arguing goodnaturedly over who would win the purple truck. They also laughed at the sequins on Wiley's orange suit.

Dark clouds had rolled in, obliterating the dwindling sunshine and casting shadows across the parking lot full of used-car bargains, but the looming bad weather hadn't deterred the crowd. Nearly everyone in Sugar Hill had turned out. She spotted Mimi and Seth with their baby, Hannah and Jake, and Alison and Brady, who'd just returned from their honeymoon.

Thomas was nowhere in sight.

Rebecca fought off disappointment and loneliness as she watched her cousins with their new husbands and their father. Wiley was boisterous and loud and might look foolish, but the children who'd shown up loved his corny jokes, and his daughters loved him. He didn't seem to act differently toward any of the girls, either.

She spotted Jerry hitching up his pants as he loped toward the cotton candy machine.

"I'll be right back," she told Gertrude, who'd settled in one of the folding chairs around a makeshift stage to listen to the country-and-western band and watch the local cloggers.

Jerry's ruddy face sparked with a grin as she approached.

Just be short, sweet and get it over with, Rebecca silently told herself.

"Hey, Bec." Jerry licked a hunk of cotton candy into his mouth. "I was wondering when I'd catch up with ya."

"Listen, Jerry, I can't hang out with you tonight," Rebecca said.

Jerry's smile fell. "Got somethin' better to do?"

She could only hope. "I'm sorry, Jerry." She gestured toward the woman who was oblivious to her meddling. "But Gertrude isn't busy. She was awfully lonely earlier."

"Do tell." Jerry snatched another bite of the sticky candy and shrugged. Quickly recovering from her rejection of him, he walked toward Gertrude. Feeling marginally better, Rebecca called to him and motioned for him to wipe the cottony pink stuff off his cheek before he reached her.

Then she turned and saw Thomas drive up in that yellow Mustang.

What had she told Gertrude? Go after what you want.

Maybe it was time she listened to her cousins and took the advice she'd passed on to her friend.

THOMAS HAD FINALLY GROWN tired of the business conversation at the lounge. Then Shawnee had insisted they dance. The music had been deafening, the smoke suffocating. But the woman he'd held in his arms had been good-looking, available, interested and she glided across the dance floor as if she owned it.

Unfortunately, she hadn't stirred his interests at all.

No, he'd imagined Rebecca Hartwell in his arms with her curves pressed up against him, and that soft silky blond hair tickling his chin. He had tried his best to banish the image.

But as he'd driven back to Sugar Hill, an emptiness swelled inside him. Trouble was, he couldn't figure out why. He was on the verge of having the life he wanted, the career he'd dreamed of forever. So, why didn't he feel overjoyed?

He must be suffering from exhaustion. And he was still worried about the Lackey baby.

Then he saw Rebecca standing in the midst of the small-town celebration with bright streamers draped around the used-car parking lot, country music blaring in the background and the town people socializing, laughing as their children took part in some of the games Wiley had arranged. His mood shifted, the air growing tighter around him. Rebecca stood out in a sea of women who had made it clear they wanted him.

But Rebecca told her grandmother she was against marriage, he reminded himself. That was a good thing, since he didn't want marriage or life here; he wanted to move onto bigger and better things.

She wove her way through the crowd toward him, and his senses spun at the sight of her. Again she'd ditched the baggy dress and wore tight jeans that hugged her rounded behind, and a soft violet sweater that stretched across ample breasts that swayed gently when she walked.

"Hey, Thomas."

"Hi."

The wind whistled between them in the silence.

"My car's ready," he said to break the tension. "So I'm returning Wiley's Mustang."

"Oh."

Did she sound disappointed?

"Yeah, the Porsche looks like new. It's at the garage in town."

"You need a ride to pick it up?"

"I figured one of Wiley's salespeople could give me a lift."

Rebecca smiled. "I could drive you." Then as if she remembered the last ride they'd taken after she'd wrecked his car, she hesitated. "That is, if you're not afraid."

Her words triggered a knot of anxiety that he felt in his stomach. He wasn't afraid to ride in the car with her.

But becoming more involved with her scared the bejammers out of him. After all, she'd been on his mind all day in Atlanta, even while he'd danced with that doctor.

Hell, he'd never been so poleaxed by a female before that he'd held one woman while wanting another.

"JUST LET ME MAKE SURE Gertrude has a ride home."

Thomas nodded and followed her over to her friend. Rebecca smiled; Jerry and Gertrude seemed to be hitting if off. In fact, Jerry had slung his arm along the back of her folding chair, and she had leaned into him as they swayed to a slow country tune. She tapped Gertrude and whispered an apology.

"I'm going to give Dr. Emerson a ride to his car."

"Something going on with you two?" Gertrude whispered.

I'm not sure. "I owe him, since I'm the one who wrecked his Porsche in the first place. Do you think—"

"I'll give Gertrude a lift," Jerry offered with a wink.

Rebecca grinned. "Great."

A flutter of nerves attacked her as Thomas followed her to her station wagon. Of course, she sensed half the town's single women giving her the evil eye. She was sure they all wondered what Thomas Emerson was doing with her.

Stop that, she ordered herself, remembering the positive talk she'd read about in the self-help book she'd bought last week. *Go after what you want.*

And I want Thomas.

"H..." She paused and took a deep breath to keep from stuttering. And to keep herself from driving like a maniac. "Hannah said you had a seminar in Atlanta."

He fastened his seat belt. "Yes, it was really interesting." He filled the next five minutes describing some of what he'd learned.

"Wow, it sounds fascinating. I read an article on

stem-cell research the other day and found it amazing."

They talked for several minutes about the research, then he confided about visiting the Lackey baby. "He survived the first surgery but only time will tell about his prognosis."

Emotions strained his voice, and she instinctively reached out and squeezed his hand, which sent shards of sensations flitting through her. He seemed to stiffen, though, and she pulled away, unsure he welcomed her overture.

"Dr. Zimmerman, one of the leading doctors in fertility treatments, spoke yesterday," he said.

This was her moment. She should ask him now about donating sperm. Only, after that kiss, could she settle for an impersonal donation?

"I don't understand this trend for single women to have babies on their own, though. It's understandable when a spouse dies or there's a divorce, but to choose to bring a baby into the world without a father..." He shrugged. "I'm not sure it's fair to the child."

She tightened her fingers around the steering wheel. Maybe he was right. Maybe it wouldn't be fair of her to have a fatherless baby. "But not every woman finds the right man to marry," Rebecca argued. "Or wants to get married."

"That's true. What do you have against marriage, Rebecca?"

She was shocked by the question. "N-nothing, really. B-but I'm not sure it's for me." What else could she say? *I want to get married, Thomas, and I think you'd make the perfect husband. I have my bride's book ready, now all I need is my bridegroom.* "A lot of men today have commitment problems. And look at my father. He's been married four times and the last two barely lasted a year."

He twisted his mouth sideways in thought, then surprised her by changing the conversation to the weather. It was almost as if they were strangers. As if he had never shown up at her house that night and bared his soul about the baby. As if he had never kissed her and almost taken her to bed.

He gripped the door handle when she stopped and swung open the door, ready to climb out. "Thanks for the ride, Rebecca."

She nodded, even more confused by the conflicting heat flaring in his eyes.

Then the wind brought a cloud of some strong odor toward her, and she realized it was perfume. A *woman's* perfume.

No wonder he was in such a hurry to get away from her. He had obviously been with another woman tonight.

Chapter Twelve

Thomas felt like a jerk as he sped toward his house in his Porsche. He had been so cold to Rebecca, but he had to put some distance between them.

Some much-needed *emotional* distance.

After all, miles would separate them when he moved, just as their needs and goals in life separated them now. And he didn't want to hurt her, so he couldn't lead her on or let her believe that they might have a future together. He could never bring his baby brother back, but in Atlanta he could save others. As long as he had the skills he needed to do so. And the equipment and technology and staff. Sugar Hill had none of that. So he didn't really belong here.

Yet deep inside his chest that emptiness returned, that aching and yearning for something more.

Why? What was it he wanted that he wouldn't have in Atlanta?

Rebecca fitted perfectly into that small-town celebration. She would not be comfortable at charity fundraisers and entertaining hospital board members, all part of the trimmings he'd need for a wife.

Wife?

Was he really considering marrying Rebecca?

No. He wasn't ready for that kind of commitment. They'd never officially even dated.

So, why had he been so upset when she'd spoken up adamantly against the institution?

Shaken by the direction of his thoughts, he pulled into his garage and went into the house. The empty rooms greeted him with silence, the sterile odors of cleaner and expensive woods almost stifling. He roamed through each room, trying to decide whether or not he liked the modernist artwork and decor the decorator had chosen. There were no photos of family or friends, no homey touches like the ones Rebecca had crammed into that tiny little place of hers. That place should feel stifling, not his.

But in his mind he saw the tulip garden Rebecca had painted, the lush mountain greenery, the gazebo up on Pine Mountain where all her cousins had married, the vibrant colors and the passion she interjected in each piece.

Was that what was missing from his house? The passion...

And what about his life?

No, he had passion for his work. Like the other doctors he'd met tonight, that was all the passion he had time for.

Determined to prove that his work still satisfied him, he headed back to his car. New Year's Eve or not, he'd stop by the clinic and pick up a few of the medical journals he hadn't had time to read yet. Might as well accomplish something on New Year's Day.

Out with the old and in with the new—and onto a new life.

Medicine was all that mattered, wasn't it?

REBECCA WORKED ON THE waterfall scene, well aware she was using her art as an escape. She'd been so rattled after she'd left Thomas she hadn't been able to eat, but she'd stopped by the celebration in the park and bought one of the picnic dinners just to support the town. The uneaten food still sat on the table at the clinic.

She should forget about this crazy attraction to Thomas. Tomorrow would be the start of a new year, her resolution would be to forget him.

Still, knowing Thomas had commissioned her to paint the murals for the clinic, that he roamed the halls of this building and spent his days here, that she could smell the lingering scent of his cologne in the empty hallways drove the knife deeper into the pain she felt from his earlier dismissal.

Something had changed since his trip to Atlanta, but she didn't understand what.

Except that it involved another woman who reeked of some expensive French perfume. Someone obviously much more experienced and sophisticated than her.

Her hand slipped, the brush strayed, and glittery white paint streaked down into the sea of blue she'd chosen for the pool of water at the base of the waterfall. Drat.

At least she could fix the paint.

How could she fix her heart from breaking over a man who obviously didn't want her?

She glanced at the desk where *The Pregnancy Bible*

lay open and another wave of pain assaulted her. There was no way she could ask Thomas to help her with her baby plan now.

Maybe it would be easier to visit a sperm bank and talk to a stranger, anyway. Someone who wouldn't judge her or think she was desperate. Or worse, look at her with pity.

An idea struck, and she rushed to the front desk, turned on the computer, then checked for fertility clinics and sperm donor centers in Atlanta. When she located one, she logged on and sent an e-mail asking the clinic to mail her information. It wouldn't hurt to read up on the procedure before she went for a consultation.

And if it didn't work out, no one would ever know.

THOMAS COULDN'T BELIEVE IT when he saw Rebecca's car parked at the clinic. It was almost midnight. What was she doing here?

Hell, it was dark and cold, someone might see her here and try to break in. The mere possibility sent his blood racing through his veins. Angry with her for being so foolish, he hurriedly let himself into the clinic.

Not certain which room she was in, he checked the first two and saw the dinosaur mural, then the jungle one. Wow. The colors certainly brightened up the exam areas; she had done a fabulous job. He still didn't understand why she didn't show her work to others.

He found her in the fourth room, completely immersed in the details of a gorgeous waterfall that pooled into a crystal-blue stream on the side of a mountain. Pure heaven.

"Rebecca?"

She shrieked, then jerked around and flung the paintbrush at him, as if she thought that skinny piece of wood might fend off an attacker.

"Y-you scared me." She ran toward him, reaching for a rag to wipe the white paint splattered on his pants legs. He grabbed her hand before she did too much damage.

"I'm sorry I frightened you, but you shouldn't be here this time of night alone."

"I was...w-working," she stammered.

He tightened his grip on her hand. "Don't you know how dangerous it is for a woman to be here at night by herself?"

"I thought the door was locked."

"It was. I have a key."

Her big blue eyes met his. "But you aren't going to hurt me."

A loaded question. He met her gaze and saw the remnants of what he thought might have been tears glistening in her eyes. Was it already too late?

Had he already hurt her?

He'd never meant to.

"Besides, you're here alone."

So, he was slightly sexist when it came to safety. Out of the corner of his eye, he caught sight of the uneaten picnic dinner for one, and his throat went dry.

He'd eaten with dozens of people around him all week but he'd still felt lonely.

She lowered her gaze and began to fidget, and his heart tugged. Unable to stand her distress, he tucked a strand of her silky hair behind one ear. Just the simple contact drove him insane. Especially when her breath hitched out in a throaty sound and the passion in her eyes echoed the passion in her paintings.

Like that rose opening its petals toward the sun, he felt her opening up toward him....

That empty hole inside him throbbed. The clock struck midnight. New Year's Eve.

He had wondered who she would be kissing at midnight. He'd wanted it to be him.

He might be leaving soon, but he had to taste her once again.

Forgetting his earlier resolve to avoid her, he lowered his mouth and allowed her to assuage the aching void inside him. And when he kissed her, he suddenly felt as if he were coming home.

Rebecca sank into Thomas's arms, thoroughly confused by his actions but totally mesmerized by the hunger in his kiss. He drove his mouth over hers in a frenzy of need, then dragged her up against his body, molding her into the vee of his thighs, and rubbing his hard length along her stomach so that she moaned and clung to him.

She wanted him to take her all the way to heaven and back this time.

His hands combed through her ponytail and snaked down her face to her shoulders, then lower to cup her buttocks and grip her hard against him. Warmth pooled in her belly and floated upward in a spiral of desire that left her dizzy.

"God, Rebecca, you taste like the sweetest of sins," Thomas growled in her ear.

The smile that radiated from her mouth originated straight from her soul. She kissed his jaw, ran her fingers along the strong set to his chin, then nibbled at his neck, giggling softly when the thick dark stubble of his beard scraped her neck. His own need escalating out of control, he dipped his head and tasted her neck. His breath licked her skin as his hands found her breasts and kneaded them through her sweater.

She had never allowed a man to see her naked before, but she suddenly craved to feel his touch everywhere.

He seemed to have the same idea.

His hands reached to the bottom of her sweater, and she slid her hands along his muscular arms and down his chest, which hardened beneath her touch.

Her rear end suddenly collided with cold metal. He jerked his gaze up and met her eyes, the passion in his look so wild and feral she lost her breath. Then he looked down and saw the exam table behind her and his look of desire changed to disgust.

"What the hell are we doing?"

The harshness of his words hit her like a slap in the face. She stiffened and bit down on her lip to stem the cry of disappointment. What had she done wrong?

He shook his head in regret, then dropped his head forward into his hands and stepped back from her. The cold metal pressed into her back as she gathered her control.

"I'm sorry, Rebecca. I..." His voice was so hoarse she could barely hear him. "I practically attacked you. And in here of all places."

He gestured around the exam room as if he'd committed a cardinal sin.

"You didn't do anything I didn't want," she said in a surprisingly strong voice. "In case you didn't notice, I wasn't fighting you."

His hands fell to his sides, and his clear green eyes met hers, turmoil and regret and hunger warring together. "This is no place for—"

For her first time? He couldn't know, could he? "To make love."

He hissed out a breath. "For sex."

The bluntness of his words stabbed at her insecurity. "Right." But she refused to allow him to see how much he'd hurt her. Instead she lifted her chin and gathered her purse. She had to get out of there before she disintegrated into tears and unleashed the foolish words threatening to erupt.

He grabbed her by her arms and forced her to face him. "I don't want to hurt you, Rebecca." His voice was hard, gravelly. "I can't deny that I want to be with you. But..."

"But what, Thomas?"

"But I can't make any promises."

She stared at him long and hard. A heartbeat of silence stretched into eternity.

"Is that what you think I want?"

"I don't know." He shook his head, yanked his keys from his pocket and gently coaxed her toward the door. "But it's what you deserve. And I can't take you here like I'm some horny high schooler."

She allowed him to lead her into the chilly night air. Snow fluttered down from a darkening sky, creating a soft blanket of white on the tops of the cedars and pines. But the breeze brought the scent of that French perfume again.

This time disgust filled her.

Didn't she have any pride? How could she have

crawled all over him, been ready to make love with him, when he had just left another woman?

BY NOON THE NEXT DAY, Thomas had enough food for an army. Everything from black-eyed peas and collard greens to fried chicken and homemade apple pie. But not one dish had come from the woman he'd left behind the night before.

What had he been thinking, almost making love to Rebecca in an exam room with a metal table pressing into her back?

He hadn't thought, he realized. He'd simply been reacting. Letting his body think for him.

Rebecca might hate him now for his abrupt withdrawal, but when he left town, she would be glad he hadn't followed through and taken her to bed. Then some other man would be her lover....

He pumped the weights harder, desperately trying to alleviate his anxiety and purge himself of the irrational jealousy the images brought. His body ached from lack of sleep and his unsated desire for her, but he hadn't been able to rest last night after he'd left Rebecca.

Had she dreamt of holding him the way he'd dreamt of sleeping with her in his arms?

REBECCA WOKE FROM a deep sleep and sat up, her body shimmering with perspiration. She glanced around the dark bedroom to make certain she was alone. That she had indeed been dreaming.

Of course she'd been dreaming.

She'd been in Hawaii on a moonlit beach with a

thousand stars glittering above an inky sky. And she'd been doing the hula dance completely naked.

In front of Thomas.

Pulling her velour robe around her, she glanced at the hope chest and wondered if her dream had any significance, if the hope chest had somehow triggered these wild dreams she'd been having.

Curious, she scanned the book on dream analysis until she discovered two notations. According to the book, dreaming about being naked was supposedly a good omen.

"Performing the undulating dance form of the hula means you'll have exciting romantic adventures in your future."

In light of the night before and her close encounter with Thomas, she laughed at the dream interpretation.

Confused and still tingling from wanting him, she lay back on her pillows and tried to plan her day. It was a new year. She should set her goals. Start over with a fresh attitude.

The sooner she finished the murals the better. Then she wouldn't have to see Thomas any more and be tempted to beg him to finish what they'd begun.

Her heart squeezed at the thought of never having his lips touch her again. Of never having his hands trail over her.

The phone rang and she stared at it for a long moment. Maybe Thomas would suggest they meet and continue their romantic interlude from the night before.

No, it was Suzanne.

"I hope your New Year's Eve was better than mine," Suzanne said.

Suzanne sounded as if she'd been crying.

''What's wrong?''

''Nick.''

''I thought you two already broke up.''

''We did.'' Suzanne sniffed. ''But we've been on again for a couple of days. It's definitely over now.''

Rebecca pulled at a loose thread on the afghan at her feet, weaving it back into the pattern. She only wished she could smooth out her own problems as easily. ''Did you love him, Suzanne?''

Suzanne sighed. ''I don't know what I felt. But I'm so tired of the dating game. And my job...it's so demanding.'' Another long sniffle. ''You're so lucky to be living in that small town. You have Hannah and Mimi and Alison there. Everyone knows you and loves you. I bet that doc is already planning to propose.''

Ha! ''I wouldn't say that.''

''Why not? Didn't you two get together?''

''Not exactly.'' Rebecca sighed. ''Look, I'm not like you. You're good with men. For heaven's sakes, you've been entertaining Dad's colleagues since you were a teenager.''

''I only took over the entertaining because you hated it,'' Suzanne said.

Rebecca frowned into the phone. She had hated it, but she'd always assumed Suzanne enjoyed the attention.

''It was obvious you were mortified by all those people in the house,'' Suzanne continued, ''but you were great in the kitchen, so I just jumped in and did what I do best. Talk.''

Rebecca laughed. ''You are good at conversation.''

''Yeah, so why can't I hold a guy?''

They both lapsed into silence. Rebecca felt a closeness to her sister she hadn't felt in years. Why had she spent so much time being jealous of Suzanne?

"Now, tell me about Thomas." Suzanne made an exaggerated sound. "I know he has the hots for you. What on earth is holding you back?"

For the first time in her life, Rebecca told her sister her problems. Relaying the painful story from the night before only magnified her doubts, though. "He keeps getting close, then pulling away. I don't know how to handle the situation."

Suzanne let the silence linger for a minute. "Well, if you want my advice, you should go after him. He probably thinks you won't sleep with him without a ring on your finger, and he's not ready for a commitment yet."

She would like a ring and a commitment. But heck, she'd almost given in to passion in an exam room the night before. "He did say he can't make any promises."

"There you go. You need to be assertive, Rebecca. Let him know you want him and that you'll accept the relationship on his terms for now." She whistled. "Of course, sooner or later, you'll warm him to marriage, but just let him know you're not pushing too hard too fast."

"But I thought I did that last night, then he started acting all noble."

"Seduce him," Suzanne said matter-of-factly. "Be bold about it. Show up wearing nothing but a raincoat. Then he can't possibly turn you down."

Rebecca wasn't so sure.

"Oh, and don't forget to take protection. The last thing you want to do is end up pregnant."

Chapter Thirteen

She didn't want to end up pregnant?

How little her sister understood her, Rebecca thought, as she primed herself with Suzanne's encouraging words while she worked on the mural. By dinner she'd nearly completed the waterfall scene and rallied her confidence and determination.

It was a new year. The beginning of a new attitude. The start of a new life for her.

A new Rebecca was emerging.

Out with the shy, dowdy girl and in with the bold, go-after-what-you-want woman!

So, why was her stomach sitting in her throat and her knees shaking so badly she thought they might literally pop in two like thin twigs?

Because she was naked beneath her dark-blue raincoat, and she was sitting in front of Thomas's house, knowing he was only a few hundred feet away. And she was deathly afraid she'd make a fool out of herself and he would order her to go home where all good girls belonged.

He was such a nice, intelligent, decent man. Would he think she was crazy for doing such a drastic thing?

No, he had admitted last night he wanted her. He was trying to be honorable because he couldn't commit. She would show him that he didn't have to commit right now. That she was a modern woman, not some old-fashioned girl who required a ring on her finger before she'd let a man touch her.

She'd prove she could take a chance on a great guy like him and wait for promises of a permanent relationship. After all, would she ever find a man if she didn't take chances?

Snow fell in a light blanket around the massive brick house, dotting the thicket of evergreens and thick grass. The cloud cover painted pale-gray lines in the sky while the wind whistled a soft melody through the trees, adding to the romantic atmosphere.

Believe in yourself. Follow your dreams.

She inhaled, took a deep breath and pushed open the door. Grabbing the bottle of wine with one hand and checking for the condoms in her pocket with the other, because, although she did want a baby, she refused to trap a man without his knowledge, she wobbled on the new gold heels that Mimi had insisted she buy, up the azalea-lined sidewalk to Thomas's house. She had never been there before, but her stomach was twisting and turning so badly that she couldn't quite appreciate the porch entrance or the impressive arched doorway or the elaborate Palladian windows in front.

He lived here alone?

Passages from the erotic poetry book Grammy had given her flitted through her mind.

Hands gently gliding across bare skin, fingers teasing, lips tasting, one body offering bliss....

She wanted to experience that bliss with Thomas.

Releasing a labored breath, she raised her shaking hand and punched the doorbell.

It bellowed out like a gong, reverberating through the huge house and echoing in her mind like a siren.

Goose bumps shimmied up her arms and legs. She could not go through with this. He would take one look at her and laugh, especially when she removed her coat and he realized there was nothing beneath.

Nothing but bare flesh and a scared, lonely girl who loved him. As much as she didn't want to admit she loved him, she did.

Wishing her nerves would dissipate like the fallen snow that wouldn't quite stick to the ground, she turned to run but caught her heel in a crack between the bricks. She was stuck.

Suddenly the door swung open, and Thomas stood on the other side, wearing gym shorts and a sleeveless muscle shirt with dark hair covering his chest and legs and a light coat of perspiration dampening his glorious body.

THOMAS HAD AVOIDED answering the door all day.

He'd also avoided the clinic because he'd suspected Rebecca would be there painting. Instead, he'd read his journals and did some research on the Internet, holding thoughts of Rebecca at bay.

Now she stood on his doorstep with light snow falling around her like some kind of angelic vision that had drifted down from the clouds.

''Rebecca?''

She shivered slightly, and he realized she must be cold.

Logic warned him not to invite her in, but she

looked so damn nervous and he didn't want to hurt her feelings.

"Come in. I...I wasn't expecting you."

"I know." She lifted her hand in offering, and he immediately thought of chicken casseroles. Instead, she held up a bottle of Chardonnay. "I finished the waterfall mural and thought I'd drop you off a New Year's Day gift."

"Thanks." He took her arm to guide her inside, but she squeaked a reply, and he noticed her shoe wedged in the bricks. He stooped to loosen it, his hand brushing bare leg as he yanked her heel from the crevice. He silently groaned. Trying to forget the way her bare leg felt on his hand and the allure of those sparkly shoes, he stood and ushered her in out of the cold. What was she so dressed up for? Did she have a date after she dropped off his gift? "Can I take your coat?"

She hugged her arms around herself. "No...not yet. I'm still a little chilly."

Hell, who was he kidding? He had wanted to see her all day.

"Come over by the fireplace." He led her to the great room with its cathedral ceiling where he'd been working earlier and onto the overstuffed throw pillows on the floor by the brick fireplace. "This should warm you up."

"Thanks."

"You want a glass of that wine?"

"Sure." She darted a glance around the room. The roaring fire. The overstuffed leather sofa. The oil painting of some Civil War figure. The TV blaring a football game. What was she thinking about his lifestyle?

Did she like his house? Was she comparing it to her homey, artsy little abode? A place that was so full of Rebecca....

"Listen, I'm all sweaty from working out, let me hop in the shower while you warm up, then we can talk. Unless you were on your way somewhere. You look like you're all dressed up."

Her face colored slightly. "No, I'll wait."

He opened the bottle of wine, poured her a glass, then handed it to her, their fingers brushing. He could have sworn her hand trembled as she gripped the glass and sipped. His heart pounding, he jerked his eyes from those pink lips pressing around the rim of the glass and hurried back to his bedroom. Maybe a cold shower would wipe out his reaction to her.

But what could they discuss that wouldn't elicit images of him tearing off that raincoat and making love to her?

REBECCA CHASTISED HERSELF for not just tearing off her coat and asking him to make love to her. But she had frozen like rain in an ice storm.

Better to take it slow. Seduce him, not jump his bones and scare the poor man to death.

Trying to calm herself, she studied the huge den with its neutral decor, amazed at how perfectly everything matched. A cherry sofa table held a crystal lamp behind plush off-white leather furniture with several antique-looking books wedged between globe-shaped bookends. Throw pillows in beige, dark blue and rust stripes accented the leather, and the oil paintings on the wall and oriental vases and sculptures looked very expensive. Window dressings that had to be custom made draped Palladian floor-to-ceiling windows that let natural light spill through the room. Now, at dusk, with the dark winter clouds hovering above, a soft ebony glow filled the massive space.

Yet, except for Thomas's laptop and a few medical books spread on a corner rolltop desk, there were no personal touches of the man himself. Did he bury himself in his work to the point of not having a life, like her father had when she was growing up?

She heard the shower water running and groaned. Images of Thomas naked and wet, his body covered with soapy water and bubbles taunted her. She sipped the wine, the heat from the fireplace finally warming her chilled body.

Or maybe it was the heat of wanting Thomas.

Nerves skidding to the surface, she stood and paced to release her pent-up energy. By the time the water kicked off, she'd almost broken into a sweat.

This was a mistake. She could not go through with the seduction.

She turned, contemplating how fast she could reach the door when his voice stopped her. "What's wrong, Rebecca? You seem nervous."

She pivoted and saw him standing in the arched doorway wearing a pair of jeans that hung low on his hips and a white shirt that he hadn't yet buttoned. Heavens alive, he was impressive.

No, she was not going to run.

"I...I just don't want to impose."

The scent of his soap-cleaned masculine body tortured her as he walked closer. "You're not. I've been holed up working all day. It's nice to take a break."

"You were watching football."

"The game's over."

He hit the off button on the TV, then led her back to the pillows. She sat down on the plush mounds, hugging the glass of wine to her like a lifeline. He poured himself a glass, flipped on the stereo to some soft jazz music, then joined her, stretching out his long muscular legs, his shirt falling open. "I figured I'd use the day to catch up on my medical journals. I have to stay current."

"You really love your work, don't you?"

"I imagine the same way you feel about your painting. It's my passion."

The word hung between them, evoking images and desires that she couldn't deny any longer. As if he read her thoughts, his dark gaze skated over her, the heat from his eyes blazing a trail of hunger through her. That heat, coupled with the warmth from the fireplace, sparked a fiery need to life.

"Are you getting warm?"

His husky voice felt like velvet. "Yes. Hot."

"Can I take your coat now?"

A slow smile captured her mouth as she nodded. Then she untied the sash and watched his eyes darken as she gently slid the garment down her shoulders.

THOMAS'S BREATH CAUGHT in his throat at the sight of the satiny expanse of Rebecca's shoulders. His hands clenched around his glass as she lowered the coat even further and he realized she was wearing nothing beneath.

Soft plump breasts jutted forward, her rosy nipples pert and begging for his touch.

His stunned gaze swung back to her face, and he struggled to make his mouth work, but his mind couldn't assimilate what was happening. What she might be offering.

Although she tilted her head up as if she had done this a million times, he noticed the slight quiver of her lips as they parted, the painful hitch of her breath as she waited for his response. He had never seen anything so beautiful as her fake bravado.

Or the bare flesh before him and the purest of hearts that beat inside that luscious, naked skin.

God help him but he couldn't refuse her invitation.

Still, he tried.... "Rebecca—"

"Shh." She raised a long, slender finger and pressed it to his lips. "You s—" She hesitated and cleared her throat. "You said last night that you wanted me but that you couldn't make any promises."

He closed his eyes to the sound of blood roaring in his ears. "I still can't."

She traced her finger along his lips in the most exquisite erotic gesture he'd ever felt. "I'm not asking for promises, Thomas. I'm just asking for tonight."

He opened his eyes, knowing he had the perfect reason to stop this insanity now. "But I don't have protection."

A blush rose on her cheeks as she gestured at her pockets. "It's taken care of."

He searched her face for hesitation, for anxiety. But just like the Rebecca he'd come to know, to like, to trust, he saw only honesty. No hidden agendas. No lies. No conniving or flirting.

Just simple, honest emotions and a hunger in her eyes that destroyed every last bit of his crumbling resistance.

REBECCA CLOSED HER EYES and just felt....

Every touch, every moment his mouth devoured her

was an erotic journey she had never embarked on before. Once he unleashed his passion, the storm of his need swept her up into a tailspin of her own primitive want. He ravaged her mouth and stroked and tortured her with his fingers and lips until she nearly cried out with the sensations flooding her body. Finally he shucked off his shirt and jeans and allowed her to touch and explore his body. Taut muscles. Sinewy strength. Masculinity so raw and tough yet so gentle and sweet.

She had never imagined being so bold. But verses from that erotic poetry book hummed through her mind, the touches, the loving gestures that brought moans from deep within his throat and had her own body clenching and pulsing with the desire to be complete.

With him.

She had no hesitation.

But she saw the shock on his face when he plunged himself inside her. He froze, muscled arms shaking as he braced himself above her.

"Rebecca, oh..." The dark passion in his eyes turned tender, then he started to pull away.

"No, please, Thomas." She grasped his hips, felt the strength in his body and wanted his possession. "I want you so much. Please."

His gaze locked with hers, filled with heat and savage hunger. His breath rattled, filled with turmoil. Then he swallowed hard. She cupped his jaw in her hands, pulled his face toward her, then gently licked his lips until he allowed her to explore his mouth. As she played deeper and deeper into the hot darkness that fueled her own needs, his resistance faded, and he finally claimed her in the most elemental way a man could, forming an intimate connection that seared her soul.

She kissed him fiercely, with all her love, then groaned his name as he took her to heaven.

A FEW MINUTES LATER Thomas lay back with Rebecca curled into his arms, his body still quaking with ecstasy from their lovemaking. But his mind was a total mess.

He had never experienced anything so tender and emotional, yet primal at the same time.

"What the hell happened?"

"New Year's resolution. To be a different woman."

"Really? And to think mine was to pay my taxes on time." He brushed a tendril of hair from her forehead, then twirled it in his finger, his gaze raking over her. "And what prompted this resolution?"

Rebecca laughed softly against his chest and turned that innocent-looking face up toward him. Baby-blue eyes blinked and sparkled with pleasure. Pleasure he had given her. "The hope chest started it all."

"What?"

Her dainty shoulders shrugged beneath him. "The things inside, the letter from Grammy—"

"Your *grandmother* wrote you a letter telling you to come over here wearing nothing but a raincoat?"

"No." She laughed again, a soft musical sound full of womanly wickedness that aroused him even more. "But she did give me a book of erotic poetry that sparked some ideas."

In spite of the little voice inside his head telling him to stop now, not to ask about that erotic poetry, he nuzzled her neck, feeling humbled and whole and completely enamored with her. The shy little vixen. "Maybe you could read some of that poetry to me."

She moved above him, her silky hair brushing his chest as she murmured, "'Go gentle over my body, your fingers trace a path, your flesh wanting mine…'"

Moved by the sound of her seductive voice, he mimicked her words with his touches, and loved her all over again. And this time when they rode the crest together, he could have sworn he'd died and gone to heaven.

Chapter Fourteen

The next week was the happiest week of Rebecca's life. She worked at the bookstore all day, finished the paintings at the clinic in the evening and spent heavenly nights with Thomas.

"Yo, Bec."

Rebecca had just stepped outside to walk to work and couldn't ignore Jerry. Besides, Gertrude had been gushing about him all week, and Rebecca wanted to see if the attraction was one-sided.

"How's it going, Jerry?"

He kicked at a loose rock with the toe of his dirty boot. "I, uh, wanted to tell you thanks."

"For what?"

A half grin laced his face. "For turnin' me down on New Year's Eve."

A gust of wind blew Rebecca's hair into her face. "Really?"

He stuffed his hands in the backs of his pockets, big belly jiggling. "See, the way I figure, if we'd got together, then me and Gertrude wouldn't of." The smile on his face screamed male.

"So, you really like her?" Rebecca asked.

He nodded. "She's somethin' else."

"Be good to her, then." Rebecca grinned and headed down the sidewalk. Love must be in the air. Hers had certainly grown for Thomas.

Although he hadn't said he cared for her and she certainly hadn't used the *L* word, she sensed he had feelings for her. His touch, his look, his lovemaking, all held so much tenderness and passion, and sometimes he looked at her with such reverence, her insides quivered. Other times she'd catch him watching her, staring, and she felt as if she were living in a dream that might end any second....

At night, they listened to music, and sometimes she read the erotic poetry to him by candlelight. And they always wound up making love, then she'd curl into his arms and sleep with his breath feathering against her neck and his big arms holding her tight.

Inspired by her new euphoria, she'd plunged into a new art project, a completely different take on her usual landscapes. She was painting a bed of lilies on the mountainside with two lovers intertwined, lying amongst the white petals. Although the bodies were simple outlines, the faces not visible, the man's body was definitely Thomas's.

Although, last night she'd woken in the middle of the night with an awful premonition that things were about to end. She'd also dreamt about a pair of clogs. According to the dream book, dreaming about wearing, owning or buying a pair meant you were going to have a passionate but short-lived love affair.

The passionate part she had.

Would it be short-lived?

No, she was just being paranoid.

Nothing could burst her bubble of happiness. She'd even stalled talking to the people at the sperm donor clinic in hopes that things would work out for her and Thomas. Then she could have a family the old-fashioned way, with the man she wanted.

Friday was Grammy's party. The whole family would be together. She'd decided to wear the violet dress she'd bought on the shopping trip with her sister and cousins. Then she would surprise Thomas with a room at the Honeysuckle Inn and they could have a romantic night together.

Nothing could go wrong now.

IT HAD BEEN THE BEST and worst week of Thomas's life.

Turmoil gripped him every time he thought of Rebecca. During the day when he was immersed in work, he reminded himself to end their relationship, to let her down gently, to break it off so he could move to Atlanta and not hurt her.

Then she would walk into a room, and all that sweetness and bright sunshine that surrounded her like a halo would burst into the dark emptiness of his soul and his intentions evaporated like rainwater on the hot pavement.

He would not only forget his intentions, hell, he'd take her in his arms and make love to her until neither one of them could breathe.

He dropped his head in his hands and tried to gather his composure, then took a deep breath and knocked on Sonya Farris's hospital room door. He'd just finished delivering twins at the hospital; he shouldn't be thinking about Rebecca. He should be thinking about work.

Her husband called, "Come in."

He smiled as he entered. "How's the new mother doing?"

"Great." She looked exhausted but happy. Even when they'd resorted to the emergency C-section, the thirty-year-old woman had been a trooper. "I can't wait to hold the babies again."

Her husband looked worse than she did as he stood by her side. He stuck out his hand. "I can't thank you enough, Doc." The man's voice broke and tears filled his eyes. "Me and Sonya wanted a baby forever. Now you give us two."

"Your wife did all the work," Thomas said, touched by the man's emotions.

Mr. Farris nodded, pinching the bridge of his nose with his fingers. "Yeah, she's amazing. But I was scared there, Doc, when things started happening. If you hadn't been there, things could have really gone wrong."

Thomas shrugged off the praise. "I simply did what any doctor would do."

"No, Doc, you've been more than a doctor. You've been a friend. You kept us both going these past few months when we were worried the twins would come early." He cleared his throat as emotions gripped him again. "I don't think we could have survived without you."

"I'm just grateful the babies are here and all right." Thomas shook the man's hand again, then promised to check on her later, but his chest ached as he left, and he contemplated the man's words. The doctors he'd met at the seminar claimed they barely knew their patients' names. Was he really making a difference here in this small town?

He enjoyed knowing his patients and their families and seeing the babies he delivered later when he passed the young mothers on the street. Would he miss that personal involvement when he worked at the Atlanta practice?

Rebecca's face flashed into his mind. They were leaving for her grandmother's party tomorrow, and his interview was scheduled for next week. He would find a way to tell her about his plans after the party.

An image of Rebecca lying in a hospital bed, hugging an infant to her breast, singing the baby a lullaby, flashed into his mind, and his breath left his lungs.

Once he left town, would Rebecca find someone else to fill her evenings—and her bed? A man who would give her a baby and convince her that marriage could work for her, even though her father's hadn't?

"OH, MY!" two of the elderly women from the church screeched as they toddled across the bookstore. "We were in the doctor's office yesterday to see Hannah," Myrtle Baker said, "and those murals you painted are wonderful, Rebecca. Why didn't you tell everyone you were so talented?"

"I...I don't usually show my work to anyone," Rebecca said, surprised by their reactions.

"My daughter Wilamina's having her first baby in the spring. Will you paint something like that for her nursery?" Delores Coggins asked.

Rebecca shrugged. "Maybe."

"How about some dancing kittens or dolls?" Delores waved a bejeweled hand. "They know it's goin' to be a girl."

"Lawdy-mae, things have sure changed haven't they?" Myrtle exclaimed. "People know the sex of their baby before it even gets here."

Rebecca laughed and promised she would consider the commission work. Oddly, the rest of the afternoon passed much the same. Word had spread about her artwork, and half the town had come in to praise her. Trudy Rodgers at the middle school invited her to talk to the schoolkids about ideas for painting a mural on their cafeteria walls. And Lynette Porter tried to enlist her to paint a backdrop for the local art theater's performance in the summer.

She couldn't wait to tell Thomas. Thanks to him, she had never felt more a part of the town.

ON THE WAY HOME, Thomas stopped by the clinic to check his messages. The usual phone calls from two nervous expectant mothers claimed a few minutes, then he checked his e-mail. A message from a sperm clinic in Atlanta came up and he read it, his mind spinning.

It was obviously a reply to a request for information: Dear Ms. Rebecca Hartwell, the information you requested is in the mail. Please let us know if you'd like to schedule a conference to discuss our services.

Thomas pushed back the chair and stared at the message. Why had Rebecca requested information about a sperm donor clinic? Was she planning to use their services?

His heart pounded as he mentally reviewed their

conversation about single mothers. She had been suspiciously silent.

And she'd told her grandmother she was against marriage. In fact, not once during the time they'd been together had she pushed for more between them. She had come to him that night to sleep with him, had claimed she didn't expect promises.

A thought stunned him.

No.

Rebecca was sweet and loyal and had no secret agendas. She would never use him to have a baby. Would she?

No, she was not like his mother....

Struggling with emotions he didn't understand—anger, hurt, fear—he printed the e-mail and stuffed it in his briefcase. He was a doctor; he would not jump to conclusions. He would do the intelligent, mature thing and calmly ask Rebecca about the note.

Surely she had some logical explanation.

REBECCA SENSED SOMETHING was wrong the minute Thomas walked into her apartment. Even his kiss felt stiff as he greeted her. She had been adding the finishing touches to the painting and quickly hid it so he couldn't see the work.

If he ever confessed his love for her, maybe she'd give it to him as a surprise.

"Have you had dinner?" she asked.

He nodded. "I grabbed something at the hospital."

She poured him a glass of wine and coaxed him to her sofa, then sat beside him with her feet curled up beneath her. "What's wrong, Thomas? Did you have a problem delivery? Is the Lackey baby all right?"

His gaze rose to meet hers. "No, the Farris twins arrived fine. And the Lackey baby is actually doing better."

"That's all good news, then." So what had him so uptight?

She waited silently, her heart pounding in her chest. He rose, then removed a sheet of paper from his briefcase. His expression was troubled as he handed it to her, his eyes solemn.

"This came today."

Rebecca took the paper and read it, a feeling of doom mushrooming in her stomach. She hadn't expected the clinic to reply by e-mail, just send the information.

"What's going on, Rebecca?"

Panic gripped her at the sound of his cool tone. She couldn't lose Thomas now, not when things were going so well between them. Not when she loved him and had hoped he might be falling in love with her.

"Why are you checking out sperm donor clinics?"

"It...it's for a friend." Lord forgive her for the lie.

His eyes narrowed. "A friend?"

She nodded, half avoiding his gaze. "From the b-bookstore. She...she asked me if I knew anything about the process."

"Is this woman having trouble getting pregnant?"

"It's an odd situation," she said, drumming her nails on her leg. "But I promised I'd keep our conversation confidential. I...shouldn't have used your computer at work, but one night I was there painting and saw those books you have and remembered her questions so I...I just sent the e-mail."

His troubled look faded slightly. "Well, if she asks

again, tell her to come and talk to me. I'll be glad to advise her."

Rebecca's guilt mounted. She had never been dishonest in her life. Yet she'd never had such high stakes that depended on her answer.

And she didn't want to lose Thomas.

Thomas couldn't explain the relief that washed over him at Rebecca's answer. He'd known she was too good, too honest to ever lie to him or do something underhanded.

Not his sweet, loving Rebecca.

But for a minute he'd thought she had, and the pain had been excruciating.

Because he cared for her…*really* cared.

He cupped her face in his hands, memorizing each delicate feature. "You are the most beautiful woman I've ever known." And she'd been a virgin. *His* virgin.

Tears glittered in Rebecca's eyes.

He kissed them away.

Then he slowly stripped her clothes and kissed every inch of her. And when she cried out his name in ecstasy this time, the fear and pain he'd experienced earlier faded, and he was almost certain that he'd fallen in love.

Trouble was, what was he going to do about it?

IN THE EARLY HOURS of morning, Thomas turned on his side and studied Rebecca's sweet sleeping form. She'd curled into him all night, and he'd held her as if he could never let her go.

But he would have to soon.

Unless he could convince her to come with him

when he moved to Atlanta. But Rebecca loved Sugar Hill. Her family was here, her friends, her store. Still, she had so much talent in her artwork. Talent that she hadn't revealed to the world.

Why?

Was she afraid people wouldn't recognize the beauty in her work or appreciate it? She was wrong. He'd already heard from patients and Hannah that people loved the murals on the walls at the clinic. If they saw some of her other paintings...

If she moved to Atlanta with him, she could open a studio. She wouldn't even need the bookstore.

He sat up slowly, unable to believe he was contemplating asking her to move to Atlanta with him. But Rebecca had emerged from her shell lately. She wasn't the same shy, timid girl he'd first met. She was smart and artistic, could discuss literature and music and would adjust to life in the big city.

But what about his schedule?

She'd never complained when he'd been on call or had to leave for an emergency. And she would have her art... If she would only show it, she could probably turn her talent into a lucrative business.

An idea percolated in his head. He slipped out of bed and dressed, then scribbled her a note saying he'd left for work, that he would pick her up later tonight for the party. Then he tiptoed into her studio room, studied the paintings and found one of the smaller ones she'd finished of her grandmother's tulip garden and carried it to his car. One of the physicians he'd met at the seminar had connections to an art dealer in Atlanta. He'd ask them to show the painting and see what happened.

When it sold, Rebecca would be so surprised....

Chapter Fifteen

Rebecca hurried into Mimi's house, her nerves frayed. She was running late, and Mimi had promised to fix her hair in a fancy twist with ringlets around the edges to frame her face.

She was also still battling the guilt she felt over the lie she'd told Thomas. What had happened to her these past few weeks?

She had never lied in her life.

Of course, she'd never been so bold as to go to a man's house and seduce him before, either. Maybe she should have chanced that Thomas would understand the truth.

But she didn't want to lose him.

''Come on in, Rebecca,'' Mimi said with a big grin. ''I hope you brought your dress and makeup with you.''

''I did.'' Except for Suzanne, who was riding down with Bert, the girls had all planned to meet at Mimi's to dress for the party.

''Look, I fixed Cosmopolitans to start the party.'' Mimi waved toward the colorful plastic glasses on the counter.

''Great.'' Hannah walked into the room holding Maggie Rose in her arms. Rebecca's heart clamored at the sight of the baby in the fluffy pink blanket.

''What do you think?'' Mimi flounced her curls. ''Cissy gave me a few highlights this morning at the Cut and Curl.''

''You look great,'' Rebecca said.

Hannah cooed at the baby while Rebecca played with Maggie's tiny fingers. ''I'm baby-sitting while she fixes your hair,'' Hannah said. ''I adore being an aunt.''

Alison waltzed into the room, grinning. ''Then I get to tend to Maggie while Hannah gets dressed.''

''Alison was telling us about her honeymoon,'' Mimi chirped. ''But, darn it, she won't share the good parts.''

''I have to have some secrets,'' Alison said with a wink. ''But it was so romantic!''

The girls all laughed and began to talk at once. Rebecca sat in the kitchen chair so Mimi could work on her hair, envious as her cousins compared wedding and honeymoon stories.

''I remember when I found that ring in my hope chest and had that crazy dream about Jake,'' Hannah said. ''I thought I was losing my mind. But then I fell in love with him.''

''And I almost freaked when I found baby items in my hope chest,'' Mimi said, reaching over to tug at Maggie Rose's toe. ''But look what happened. Now I have a great man and the most perfect little girl in the world.''

''And I have Brady, the only man I ever loved,'' Alison said dreamily. ''But when I found those annulment papers, I was afraid things weren't going to work out.'' She sighed, held out her hand and stared at her wedding ring. ''I'm just so happy it did.''

Rebecca wondered if her story would have a happy ending like theirs.

It would all depend on Thomas—after all, he still hadn't mentioned anything about love. Or commitment.

Mimi twisted strands of Rebecca's hair and fastened them with glittery pins. ''Alison, you know Rebecca's been seeing Thomas, right?''

''Hannah told me.'' Alison claimed the kitchen chair beside Rebecca. ''I'm so glad you two are dating. Thomas deserves someone wonderful, and I can't think of anyone more perfect for him than you.''

Rebecca gaped at her, her earlier worries resurfacing. ''You don't feel weird about us dating?''

''Of course not, it's fantastic.'' Alison squeezed her hands. ''You two make a wonderful couple.''

''Who knows?'' Mimi said, grabbing the can of hair spray, ''Maybe Rebecca'll be walking down the aisle next.''

''What did Grammy give you in your hope chest?'' Hannah asked.

Rebecca blushed as she described the contents.

''Erotic poetry,'' Mimi exclaimed. ''And Grammy wrote it?''

''She's full of all kinds of surprises,'' Rebecca said.

''She's going to be the one surprised tonight,'' Hannah said.

''As long as everyone behaves themselves,'' Alison added.

Mimi added a hint of hair spray, stood back and

admired the results. Rebecca couldn't believe her eyes; she looked like some kind of princess. The next few minutes they dressed and pampered each other, trading cosmetics and accessories.

"Okay." Mimi gathered them into a huddle before they dispersed. "Here's the plan. Everyone man their stations tonight. If you see any trouble brewing between our dads, intercept immediately."

The girls all saluted. Nothing could go wrong, not as long as the Hartwell girls stayed on the alert.

THE ENTIRE WAY TO Rebecca's, Thomas ordered himself to tell her about his plans to interview for the job in Atlanta. But she and her cousins were anxious about the party and their fathers, and he didn't want to add to her worries.

Or was he being a coward? Using that as an excuse not to rock the boat of the tentative bond they'd formed over the last few weeks.

Was he afraid if he asked her to move with him to Atlanta that she'd reject him?

He grabbed the corsage he'd bought and headed up the sidewalk to her door. Memories of childhood resurfaced—his mother pushing him away after she'd lost his brother. His father deserting him when his mother had said she didn't need him.

What about his needs? Why couldn't they have loved him?

Did Rebecca?

She'd never mentioned love, and she was against marriage....

Still, he stared at the welcome sign on Rebecca's door and remembered the sweet, tender way she made love to him. The painful memories faded. She couldn't fake the depth of emotions he glimpsed in her eyes when they held each other, or the passion in her paintings and in the way she touched him. She had to care for him, she couldn't love him with her body with such tenderness if she didn't have feelings for him, could she? Rebecca was too sincere for that.

He punched the doorbell, his pulse racing as she opened it. "My God, you look stunning." He'd never imagined the shy girl he'd first met metamorphosing into such an exquisite creature.

The soft violet dress hugged curves that he knew by heart yet teased him to unveil them again, right then and there. "Your hair looks wonderful," he whispered, leaning forward to nibble at her ear. "I can't wait to tear it down."

Her face flushed. "Thomas," she whispered in a throaty voice, "you are too much."

He checked his watch. "I guess there's not time."

She grinned a female grin that sent his libido surging. "Later, honey."

He laughed and handed her the corsage. "A lily for you to wear tonight."

Tears misted her eyes as he took it out and placed it around her wrist.

"Why did you get a lily?" she asked, emotions tingeing her voice.

"Because they stand for purity," he whispered. "Just like you are."

PURE?

Thomas thought she was sweet and pure and sincere, and yet she had lied to him!

For a minute after he'd given her the lily, she'd wondered if he'd seen the painting of the two of them naked and entwined.

Why hadn't she just admitted she wanted a baby from the beginning and was exploring her options?

Because she'd been such a chicken.

He would think she was hinting at commitment. After all, he'd admitted right away that he couldn't make promises to her. She'd thrown herself at him and pretended she didn't want a commitment or marriage when that was exactly what she wanted. Mercy, she'd dug herself into a hole. What was she going to do now?

THOMAS FELT SLIGHTLY out of place as the Hartwell family gathered in the Tiara Room. His own lack of family hadn't prepared him for the happy, boisterous group. Hannah, Mimi, Alison, their husbands, Rebecca, Suzanne and their twin cousins, Caitlin and Angie, along with dozen of Grammy Rose's friends, hugged and laughed as if they'd come together for a long overdue family reunion when, in actuality, they'd recently seen each other at Alison's wedding. The door squeaked open and two elderly blue-haired ladies toddled in.

One of them tapped her cane on the table edge. "She's here."

"Hit the lights," Mimi hissed. "Everyone in their places!"

Seconds later Grammy Rose entered, and they jumped up and yelled, "Surprise!"

"Oh, my word!" Grammy Rose's wide eyes glittered with joy as she scanned the crowded room of friends and family. The girls had arrived early enough to hang a Happy Birthday banner and streamers of silver and gold across the ceiling. In the midst of the gold-lace-draped table, the three-tiered birthday cake Mimi had baked sported enough candles to set the entire place on fire.

Grammy Rose wagged a bony finger at Clara Mae, her best friend. ''You sly old fox, you knew about this, didn't you?''

Clara patted her curly gray bob and tittered. ''Got you on that one, didn't we?''

Grammy Rose cackled. ''You're dern right. I thought we were going to Bingo night.''

Everyone laughed and clapped, each of the girls taking a turn to hug and wish their grandmother a happy birthday while the church ladies started the line for the buffet. Thomas spotted Wiley on one side of the room with Hannah, and Bert on the opposite with Suzanne as if the girls had posted themselves as guard dogs.

But it was Rebecca who stood out in the crowd. He couldn't take his eyes off her. She seemed radiant tonight in that violet dress, and so happy that the thought of confessing his possible move to Atlanta didn't seem like such a good idea. After all, he'd booked a room at the Honeysuckle Inn and wanted to convince her to stay the night with him.

He didn't want anything to spoil the evening for her.

THE PARTY WAS a huge success, Rebecca thought, as she watched everyone eat and mingle. Grammy Rose seemed on cloud nine.

And Thomas...she felt his eyes on her everywhere she went. His heated looks and sultry glances were driving her crazy. She'd looked forward to this party, yet now she couldn't wait for it to end so they could spend the night together. Her body tingled at the thought of what they would be doing later.

Grammy opened Rebecca's gift, a book of love poems, and laughed out loud. She clutched Rebecca's hands, then leaned over and whispered, "How are you and your young man getting along, dear?"

Rebecca blushed. "Fine, Grammy."

Her grandmother winked. "I had a feeling about him."

Rebecca laughed and Mimi handed her another gift. Her grandmother oohed and ahhed at the photo of Maggie Rose that Mimi framed for her. "There's a gift certificate to the spa in there, too," Mimi said. "You can get a facial, a pedicure, a massage, the works."

"Mercy," Grammy Rose said. "I can't wait for that!"

Hannah gave her a new quilting book. "And we have a surprise," Hannah said. "Jake and I are pregnant."

"Pregnant!" Mimi yelled.

"Oh, my word!" Grammy screeched.

Wiley pulled Hannah into a hug, and the other Hartwells joined in. Rebecca's eyes misted, her gaze meeting Thomas's over the chaos. He gave her an odd look, then glanced away.

Wiley hugged Grammy. "Happy birthday, Mom."

Grammy Rose punched his arm. "Oh, heck, son, I'm thrilled y'all are all here. Having you and Bert together and all my granddaughters is a gift in itself."

She winked. "Even if you have been keeping to opposite sides of the room."

Wiley laughed that boisterous laugh of his. "We both love you, you know that."

A twinge of sadness touched Grammy's eyes as the girls' twin cousins, Caitlin and Angie, approached. "Now about your mother?"

"We tried to get in touch with her," Caitlin said. "But we couldn't reach her."

"I tried to, as well," Wiley said. "But we don't know where Shelby took off to."

Grammy Rose shook her head. "She'll come back in due time, I reckon."

Rebecca caught the cue from Mimi and urged her to open the remaining gifts. Grammy hooted and cried and laughed as she opened gag gifts and sentimental ones.

Uncle Wiley handed her a small box. Grammy shrieked, "Look at this, it's a key!"

"To that gold convertible Cadillac you've always wanted." He hugged her. "I found one and had it restored."

"I declare, what a surprise, Wiley. I can't wait to drive it!"

Bert moved toward her and handed her another box. Grammy's gaze flitted from one brother to another. "Happy birthday, Mother."

Rebecca held her breath at the way the two men stalked around each other like two big old lions vying for the same territory.

Grammy opened the small gift box and held up a diamond necklace trimmed in rubies, then turned for

Bert to fasten it around her neck. "Thank you, son. It's beautiful."

"Always trying to buy people's affection with his money," Wiley muttered.

Bert scowled at Wiley. "Least ways I made something out of myself."

Oh, good heavens, Rebecca thought, they couldn't get into a brawl over the presents.

Wiley reared back as if to fight, and Mimi yanked him backward while Suzanne carted Bert off to the other side to put some distance between them.

Apparently, the boys had competed for their mother's attention all their lives. Trouble was, Rebecca understood the feeling. Suzanne and her father had always shared that special closeness, and she had been the outsider. Her father attempted to compensate for his lack of time with money, while Wiley took the sentimental route, which might be the reason Rebecca felt closer to him than her own dad.

She went to refresh her lemonade when she spied Thomas in the corner, deep in conversation with her father. Suzanne stood close by, stunning looking in a short, black scoop-necked cocktail dress that showcased her endless legs. Her father's voice rang out over the noisy room. "So, you have an interview all lined up with the board on Monday? Good job, Thomas," her father said. "I'll look forward to talking to the board members about bringing you on staff."

"Have you discussed leaving your practice with Hannah yet?" Suzanne asked.

Rebecca froze, lemonade sloshing over her hand as she tried to pour it from the ladle into her cup.

"Not yet, I wanted to see if things worked out

first.'' He leaned in closer. ''I'd appreciate it if you'd let me mention it to her. I'm planning to talk to her Monday morning. I wanted to wait until after the party.''

So, he intended to break up with her after the party, while she'd planned a romantic night at the Honeysuckle Inn!

Her father pumped Thomas's hand. ''All right, we'll talk more at the interview. By the way, if you're staying in Atlanta overnight, come out to my place around six. I'm having a dinner party there for colleagues and investors of the center.'' Her father curved an arm around Suzanne. ''Suzanne's agreed to come and help my new wife play hostess. She's a beauty, isn't she?''

Rebecca's heart clutched as Thomas smiled at Suzanne.

''Yes, she is. And thank you, sir, I'm looking forward to next week.'' Thomas lowered his voice, ''In fact, I'd hoped to swing an invitation to this party just to get to know you better.''

Rebecca's father chuckled. ''You'd be prepared to move to Atlanta soon?''

''Definitely,'' Thomas said. ''I'm really excited about the new medical facility and eager to see it. Sugar Hill's just not the place I want to settle.''

Rebecca let the ladle slip from her hand. Thomas was moving to Atlanta? Applying for a job because he didn't want to settle in Sugar Hill?

Meaning he didn't want to settle with her.

Not that he hadn't warned her—*I can't make any promises.*

Because he'd never intended to stay in Sugar Hill or develop a serious relationship with anyone.

Especially her.

Chapter Sixteen

Rebecca's stomach twisted, her hopes and dreams shattering into a thousand pieces. Thomas thought Suzanne was beautiful. He was moving to Atlanta and he hadn't told her or Hannah yet.

And he would be having dinner with her father and sister next week.

How could her father be so heartless as to push him toward Suzanne when Rebecca was in love with him?

Because it had never occurred to her father that his other daughter might interest someone like Thomas.

Her hand flew to her stomach. She'd wanted to have Thomas's baby so badly, but she'd wanted him, too. And they had used birth control religiously. Still, what if it had failed and she accidentally wound up pregnant, and he ended up going to Atlanta and became involved with Suzanne?

No, Suzanne wouldn't do that. She knew Rebecca had feelings for Thomas.

Memories of the other times men had used her to get to Suzanne flooded back, adding to her insecurities. What if Thomas had only been using her to get to Suzanne?

No, that didn't seem feasible. But his conversation with her father echoed in her head....

I'd hoped to swing an invitation to this party to get to know you better.

Other memories rushed back—Thomas asking her about her family. Thomas attending the seminar in Atlanta. Thomas showing up at the coffee shop just when her father and Suzanne had visited. Thomas sitting with them that day. Had he planned that impromptu meeting just to meet her father?

Had he thought dating her would put him in her father's good graces so he would offer him the job he wanted?

Pain squeezed at her lungs, threatening to cut off the air. Suddenly Wiley tapped his wineglass and called everyone around to sing "Happy Birthday" while Mimi cut the cake. Rebecca's throat clogged with tears and she ran to the bathroom, too choked up to sing.

A TWINGE OF UNEASE nagged at Thomas after his conversation with Bert. Although he appreciated the man's medical knowledge and professional reputation, it seemed as if Bert was throwing Suzanne at him. Didn't Bert realize that he and Rebecca were involved?

Rebecca wasn't very close to her father. Perhaps he had no idea...

And where had Rebecca disappeared to?

Last he'd seen her, she'd been talking to her cousins and hovering around the lemonade bowl. He excused himself from Bert and Suzanne to find her. Yet as he searched the crowded room, he didn't see her anywhere.

His anxiety grew.

Mimi pushed a piece of cake toward him, and he took it, still scanning the room. "Have you seen Rebecca?"

"I saw her duck into the powder room." Mimi waved a chocolate-coated finger where she'd scooped up a bit of icing. "She's probably in there sprucing up for you."

Thomas relaxed slightly.

"You've been good for her, Thomas," Mimi said.

He shrugged. "It works both ways." She had filled a void he hadn't even known existed.

Mimi pointed a fork at him. "Just don't hurt her, you hear me. She's too good to have her heart broken."

REBECCA'S HEART WAS BREAKING. Why hadn't Thomas told her that he was leaving?

He obviously didn't feel as if he owed her anything. All the feelings she'd imagined were just sexual ones. He'd found a willing woman who'd accept him without promises and he'd used her.

She had no one to blame but herself.

Still, he could have been honest with her.

Although she herself hadn't been up-front about her plans....

Tears trickled down her cheeks as nausea gripped her. She locked herself in the bathroom stall and let the floodgates open. Sobs racked her, even as she told herself she shouldn't be so hurt. That he hadn't exactly lied to her.

She slumped on the toilet, ripped off pieces of toilet paper, blew her nose and wiped her eyes, struggling to gain control. But another sob escaped her.

"Rebecca?"

She froze, her erratic breathing tumbling out.

"Rebecca, it's Alison, what's wrong?"

"Go away." The last person she needed to tell was Alison.

"I'm not leaving until you tell me what's wrong."

"I...please, Alison, just leave me alone."

"Rebecca."

Oh, for pity's sake, now Hannah was knocking at the stall door. "Come on, sugar, open the door."

"I— Just go b-back to the party. I'm fine."

"You are not fine," Hannah said. "Now, talk to us."

"What's going on in here?"

Lord, now Mimi. Had her cousins seen her rush in here and known something was wrong?

Rebecca dropped her head forward in her hands, shaking with humiliation.

"We're your cousins and we're here for you now, Bec," Hannah said. "Come on, let us help."

"You can't," Rebecca wailed. "I'm such a fool."

"Uh-oh, sounds like man trouble," Mimi said.

"Did Thomas say something to upset you?" Hannah asked.

"You want me to go get him?" Alison asked. "I'll drag him in here and make him explain—"

"No." Rebecca lunged up, panicked. "Please don't let him know I'm upset."

"Then open up," Mimi said.

Oh, heck, what else could she do? She couldn't very well hide in here forever.

Then she would ruin Grammy's party.

Rebecca turned the knob, knowing she looked pathetic with her red puffy eyes and smeared makeup. On a sob she spilled the entire story.

Hannah paced back and forth. "So, he's planning to leave the practice and he hasn't told me yet."

"I'm sorry, I shouldn't have told you."

"No, I'm glad you did. But he should have been the one to let me know, and he should have been honest with you."

"He never made me any promises," Rebecca said.

"I hope he's not doing this because of me." Guilt laced Alison's voice.

"Don't blame yourself," Mimi said. "This is all my fault. I pushed him toward Rebecca." Mimi's voice trembled. "Now I feel horrible."

"So do I," Hannah said.

"But you warned me this could blow up in our faces," Mimi cried. "I'll never try to play matchmaker again."

Hannah patted Mimi. "I thought he was interested and just needed a nudge, too."

Rebecca stared up at them in confusion. "What's going on?"

Hannah confessed about them coaxing him to ask her about painting the murals. So, even that hadn't been his idea.

"But I thought he really liked you, anyway," Mimi said in misery. "Honest, Bec, or we wouldn't have interfered."

"And I thought he liked it here in Sugar Hill," Hannah said. "I know he's ambitious but he acted as if he enjoyed the practice."

Rebecca hugged her cousins. "It's not your fault. I appreciate you trying to help me, though."

"I just don't understand," Alison said. "I've seen the way he's been gawking at you all night. I'd swear he's in love with you."

Rebecca shook her head. "Well, he's not. He told Dad he doesn't want to settle in Sugar Hill." And they all knew she could never live anywhere else.

"I'll talk to him," Hannah offered. "Or better yet, I'll get Jake to. Maybe he can pound some sense into him."

"No," Rebecca whispered in horror, "then he'll know I overheard."

"You want me to say something?" Alison offered.

"I've been taking kickboxing," Mimi said. "I can kick him where it hurts."

Rebecca laughed in spite of her tears. "Thanks, but no." She inhaled for courage. "Just help me repair my makeup so I can walk out there and save my pride."

The girls exchanged sisterly glances but finally nodded.

"It won't be easy not to cream him," Alison said.

"Or to hold my tongue," Hannah said.

"Or not to kick him," Mimi said, wagging her finger. "Now, listen, Bec, when the moment's right, you stick it to him or else we will." Mimi raised her head, then reached inside her purse for her makeup. "No man is going to get away with hurting one of the Hartwell girls without paying for it.''

THOMAS HAD ENGAGED WILEY in a conversation about cars, his ears burning from listening to Jake and Seth and Brady talk about the high points of marriage and having a family. Seth bragged about Maggie Rose, and Jake was thrilled that Hannah was expecting. He didn't feel comfortable joining in the conversation with the new husbands, especially with Brady giving him the evil eye as if he feared Thomas might still be harboring feelings for Alison.

He had never felt about Alison the way he did Rebecca. And he couldn't help but imagine the two of them having a baby. But if she wasn't interested in marriage, would she want a child?

''I swear all my girls have disappeared,'' Wiley said, waving a champagne glass around. ''Wonder what they're plotting?''

Thomas laughed. ''You know how girls are, they always go to the bathroom in groups.''

''Right, well, I need to find them. Some of the guests are about to leave, and they need to say goodbye.''

Thomas nodded and watched Wiley head toward the women's room, wondering if he should follow. Rebecca had been in there an awfully long time.

He certainly hoped nothing was wrong.

''WHAT'S WRONG?'' Wiley asked as all the girls exited the bathroom in a huddle.

Rebecca winced. If he'd taken one look at her and known she was upset, how would she fool Thomas and everyone else? ''Nothing.''

Wiley grabbed Rebecca's arms. "Are you sure, honey?" His gaze scrutinized her face and his eyes glazed over with horror. "There is something wrong. You've been crying."

Mimi gave him the short version.

"I told you not to tell," Rebecca hissed.

"Sorry," Mimi said with a shrug. "But Dad is family."

Hannah and Alison patted Rebecca's back. "We won't tell anyone else, don't worry."

Wiley bristled, squaring his shoulders inside his bright-purple coat. "You mean your daddy was pushing Suzanne toward Thomas when he's been dating you? What kind of fool is he?"

"Dad—" Hannah warned.

"I don't think my father has a clue," Rebecca said. "It probably never occurred to him that Thomas would like me."

"Why the hell not?" Wiley asked, his voice booming. "You're one of the prettiest girls in town."

Rebecca blushed. "Thanks, Uncle Wiley, but Dad doesn't see me that way."

"Then he's not only a fool but a blind old fool." Wiley started forward, hands clenched. "And I've got a good mind to tell him right now. He thinks money can buy everything, but doesn't he know people want love and time?"

Hannah, Mimi and Alison all grabbed him at once. "Stay out of it, Dad."

Rebecca kissed her uncle's cheek. "Thanks, Uncle Wiley, but this is my problem, not yours. And I don't want Grammy's party ruined. She was so happy you and Dad were both here."

Wiley shrugged, his red face turning ruddier.

"We're family, hon, one person's problem is everybody's."

Rebecca felt tears sting her eyes again. "Thanks, and I appreciate it, honestly I do." She dabbed at her eyes again. "But Thomas is one problem I have to take care of myself."

She gave them all a weak smile. She just had to figure out a way to end her relationship with him gracefully so he would never know he'd hurt her.

THOMAS WAS JUST ABOUT to start searching for Rebecca when she emerged from the ladies' room, her entire family in tow. Having lived alone most of his life, he envied the way the Hartwells were bonded by blood and family, sharing a closeness he'd never known.

It didn't matter, he reminded himself. He had almost everything he'd ever wanted at his fingertips. A great job in Atlanta, prestige, money, a bright future.

But would he be sharing it with the woman he wanted? Was Rebecca the right one to stand by his side and help him climb the ladder of success?

He caught her gaze, and his heart gave an odd leap at the expression in her eyes. Not the adoration he'd seen earlier, but a darker look. Wariness. Worry.

He couldn't quite read her feelings, but noting Wiley's glare toward Bert, he assumed her anxious look resulted from the two men and their ongoing feud, so he brushed off the uneasiness. He rushed toward her with a smile. The party was breaking up and he wanted to have her to himself. Alone at the Honeysuckle Inn.

At least for another night.

She met him halfway. "Thomas, I hope you enjoyed the party and weren't too bored with all this family stuff.''

''No, it was fun. Your family is charming.'' He'd accomplished everything he'd set out to do, so why did he suddenly have this feeling of impending doom. ''Are you ready to leave?''

She nodded. ''Thanks for bringing me here. But I—I've decided to go home with Grammy tonight.''

''What?'' He tempered his hurt and leaned over to kiss her. ''I thought we'd spend the night together.''

She turned slightly so his kiss landed against her cheek. ''I'm sorry. I should have said something sooner, but I didn't realize Grammy was expecting me.'' Her eyes turned pleading. ''I just don't want to disappoint her on her birthday.''

He swallowed his disappointment. He couldn't deny a seventy-five-year-old woman her birthday request, either.

Besides, it was only one night. If he worked things right, he'd have the rest of his life to spend with Rebecca.

REBECCA BARELY MADE IT through saying goodbye to Thomas without bursting into tears again. Though part of her had wanted to confront him for using her, her pride kept her from creating a scene.

Her father and uncle were a different story. With only a few minutes left, they forgot pride, and their snipping careened out of control.

''Did you have to wear such a godawful suit?'' Bert said. ''I'm surprised you didn't blind the poor hostess when you came flashing in. All those whistles and bells and lights on your car, you'd think you were some rock star.''

''Maybe if you'd strip off your snottiness, you'd realize I'm just trying to show people a good time, not buy their love.''

''You're simply jealous that I'm a success and you're not.''

''My business is doing very well,'' Wiley boasted.

''You mean those cheesy ads and corny signs you post draw in suckers for your jalopies?''

''My cars are not jalopies.''

''At least my daughters can be proud of me,'' Bert said, puffing up his chest.

''Proud?'' Wiley bellowed. ''You ignorant oaf! You dote on one daughter and ignore the other—''

''I do not.''

''You most certainly do. It's so obvious it makes me furious. I'd like to pound some sense into you—''

Mimi and Hannah and Alison grabbed Wiley's arm before he could throw a punch. Suzanne caught Bert's hand just as it formed a fist, and dragged him toward the door.

Rebecca curled an arm around her grandmother, mortified. ''I'm sorry, Gram—''

''Shh, don't fret.'' Grammy Rose laughed. ''Boys will be boys.'' Rebecca gave Thomas one last pained look as she walked her grandmother outside. Once Grammy was settled in with her friend, Rebecca sneaked into her uncle Wiley's Suburban.

She couldn't let Thomas see her riding home with her uncle instead of leaving with her grandmother. Wiley threw an arm around her and hugged her, then shifted the SUV into gear and tore down the mountain, mumbling about how idiotic Bert could be.

Rebecca huddled her arms around her waist and stared out the window, but Thomas's face was etched in her mind. The miles and bumps in the road accentuated the distance and hurt that separated them.

Chapter Seventeen

One weekend shouldn't have been so long. But it seemed to drag on forever.

Monday afternoon, as Thomas entered the medical center in Atlanta to meet Bert Hartwell and the other board members, he tried to clear his head. But his mind kept whirling with worry.

All weekend he'd attempted to concentrate on his medical journals the way he used to do before he became involved with Rebecca, but that last odd look in Rebecca's eyes haunted him.

Something had been wrong.

He just couldn't put his finger on the problem.

The fact that he hadn't talked to her for days magnified his anxiety. He missed her voice, her shy sultry smile, the way she whispered his name in the throes of passion, the way she lay curled against him in the dark of night.

He'd tried to convince himself she'd just spent the weekend with her grandmother. So, why did he feel as if everything in his life had just changed? As if he'd lost her somehow?

If only she'd stayed with him at the inn that night

and he could have held her in his arms, he would have known everything was all right.

Since when did you get so dependent on a woman, Emerson? Or anyone else.

Work had always been all that mattered. It should be all that mattered now. People's lives, *babies'* lives, depended on him being his sharpest, most focused, on him knowing every possible thing that could go wrong and being able to read the situation and data correctly during a pregnancy and delivery.

Yet he hadn't been able to read Rebecca's thoughts at all.

Hannah, on the other hand, had been an open book. She'd told him she was disappointed he was considering leaving, but wished him well. Odd, but he'd actually expected her to ask him to stay.

Not that she couldn't find a replacement, but she'd been slightly distant, a little quieter than usual. Maybe she just didn't understand his ambition, his drive.

He stepped up to the receptionist's desk, excitement warring with worry. Once he firmed up his plans, he'd drop by the art studio and check on that painting of Rebecca's to see if the dealer liked it. Then, after Bert's dinner party, he'd drive straight back to Sugar Hill and see Rebecca. They needed to have a long, serious talk about their future.

REBECCA GATHERED the children around for story hour, knowing her own dreams for a future with Thomas had disintegrated this past weekend. Thank heavens he'd gone to Atlanta today and would be moving soon. At least she wouldn't have to face him every day and be tortured by his handsome face and the fact that he'd made a fool out of her.

"Okay, kids, I'm going to read you one of my favorite stories." Rebecca held up *The Ugly Duckling.* "My grandmother used to read me this one when I was little. Listen very carefully..."

When she finished the story, the children clapped.

"I wike the duckie," one of the four-year-olds said.

"I wanna be a swan," Tonya, a tiny five-year-old whispered.

"You will be," Rebecca assured her with a hug. Thomas had made her feel like the beautiful swan.

At least for a little while.

So she couldn't be too angry with him, could she?

She sang a few songs with the children, then herded them over to Mimi, who'd planned to decorate duck cookies with them in the activity corner. But Rebecca was too melancholy to join in; she simply sat and watched, her heart heavy. Maybe she'd overreacted....

Gertrude tapped her on the shoulder. "You have a phone call."

Please not Thomas. "Who is it?"

"A man named Robertson. He's an art dealer from Atlanta."

"Hmm, I don't know him." Gertrude shrugged and Rebecca rose and went to the phone. "Rebecca Hartwell speaking."

"Hi, Ms. Hartwell, I'm delighted to speak to you, and I appreciate you giving us the opportunity to show your painting."

"My painting?"

"Oh, sorry, we must have a bad connection?" He chuckled. "The painting of the tulip garden. It's fantastic. I love your use of colors and the lines…you show a lot of depth and sensitivity in your work.''

Rebecca frowned into the phone, totally confused. ''You have my painting of the tulip garden?''

''Yes…Dr. Emerson brought it in for you.'' He hesitated, sounding confused. ''Is there a problem?''

You might say that. ''Uh, no. I just didn't realize he'd given it to you yet.'' The lying, conniving, sneaky…

''Oh, well, yes, he brought it to me last week.''

''Last week?''

''If you have any more you'd like to send, I'd be happy to show them on commission. I think they're going to fly out of the gallery.''

Rebecca chewed a thumbnail for a second. ''As a matter of fact, I do have another one for you. Give me your address and I'll ship it to you ASAP.''

''Great.'' He recited the shop name and street. ''And let me know whenever you want to come in. If we could get several of your pieces at once, we'll feature you in a special showing.''

Just what she wanted, every art critic in Atlanta coming in to criticize her work. Her very *personal* work. She'd told Thomas that, but he obviously hadn't been listening.

She hung up, furious. Why had Thomas taken her painting to a gallery without her permission?

For the money.

Was he so much like her father that he thought money was the key to everything? That all happiness hinged on financial and career success? Forget about the people and their feelings and wants…

Well, she'd fix him. She'd send that painting of him

lying naked in the lilies to the gallery. And she'd make certain the gallery owner sent him the profits when it sold.

She certainly didn't want it hanging around her house, reminding her of their romance.

Their *affair,* rather.

Romance was meant for lovers, for people *in* love.

She was the only one who'd experienced the feeling. He'd simply been using her.

And she was ready to be done with him.

THOMAS RANG THE DOORBELL to Bert Hartwell's home in Buckhead, awed at the prestigious neighborhood and Georgian-style mansion. The interview with the board members had gone as smooth as silk, and his tour of the facility proved to be more astounding than he'd imagined. Bert had already brought in some of the finest physicians in the country plus a few European specialists who would add to the impressive staff. Bert had also offered him a deal he couldn't refuse.

His dreams were about to come true.

So why did it feel like such a hollow victory?

Because he had no one special to share the joy with.

Rebecca. He wanted her with him, wanted her to be proud of him and excited and—

"Come in, sir." A butler ushered him through a massive foyer to a formal dining area where cocktails and hors d'oeuvres abounded. Servants roamed the crowd offering drinks and fancy appetizers. An attractive woman who looked to be in her midforties with a stylish chignon and enough jewels glittering on her fingers to nearly blind him, stood beside Bert. She must be the latest Mrs. Bert Hartwell.

Two of the doctors at the fertility clinic spoke to him, then he introduced himself to Irwin Jacobs, a specialist in the area of birth defects. He'd heard the man had examined the Lackey baby.

"His prognosis is good now," Jacobs said. "You made a good call in transferring him to the neonatal unit here right away, Doctor."

Thomas nodded as the man excused himself to get another drink.

"It's nice to see you, Thomas."

He nearly spilled the scotch on his suit when he glanced up to see Suzanne.

"So, are you impressed with my father's party?"

"He certainly knows how to entertain."

"Part of the job," she said in a low voice, then gestured toward the woman at Bert's side. "But at least I can fade into the woodwork. I think the new Mrs. Hartwell is going to be exactly what Dad wants."

He raised an eyebrow at her cynical tone.

"A trophy wife," Suzanne said matter-of-factly.

"You don't think love is involved?"

"There hasn't been with the others." Suzanne wrapped her fingers around the stem of a crystal champagne flute. "That's why they never last."

He sipped his drink, studying the crowd, the expensive furnishings, the obvious appearance of success.

"Dad just wants someone to look good on his arm to impress investors and his co-workers, someone who can serve and cater and help run the charities and fund-raisers that help boost him to higher positions. I fill in between wives."

"You don't like the hostess job?"

Suzanne shrugged. "I can handle it. But," she gave him a wary glance, "Rebecca, she's a different story. She always hated these big parties."

He dragged his gaze from the crowd to her, sensing that Suzanne had issued a silent warning of some type.

Then she surprised him with directness. "Does she know you're coming to work with Dad?"

He swirled the glass around and watched the amber liquid splash over the ice. "I'm going to talk to her about it when I return to Sugar Hill."

She opened her mouth to say something else, but her father suddenly summoned her. "Don't hurt her," she whispered as she headed toward the throng of men.

"I don't intend to," he said softly.

But he wasn't sure Suzanne heard him. And if she had, the dark look she tossed him over her shoulder implied she didn't believe him.

REBECCA DRAGGED HERSELF home, struggling not to think about Thomas and the fact that he was in Atlanta planning a new job and a new life without her. And that at that moment he was probably having dinner with her father and her sister.

Suzanne was probably charming the pants off him.

No...her sister wouldn't do that, not when she knew Rebecca had feelings for him.

Would she?

Jerry and Gertrude waved to her from their patio as she climbed the stairs to her apartment. "Look!" Gertrude shouted, holding out her hand.

Something shiny glittered in the fading sunlight.

"Jerry proposed! We're getting married!"

Rebecca gulped; that was fast.

Jerry shrugged and pulled Gertrude to him.

Gertrude looked so happy Rebecca waved and yelled, "Congratulations. When's the big day?"

"We're not sure. We may run off to Reno one weekend," Gertrude said over the wind. "Doesn't that sound romantic?"

Any proposal sounded romantic to her. "I'm so happy for you." Rebecca unlocked her door. "But if you decide to get married in Sugar Hill, don't forget to invite me to the wedding."

Probably the only one she would be going to anytime soon, Rebecca thought, as she rushed inside. She flipped on the light and walked straight to her studio to box up that painting and mail it. The sooner she rid herself of it the better.

Then she'd pack away that silly hope chest and her dreams of marriage with it. Poor Grammy would be disappointed that this time the magic of the hope chest hadn't worked.

THOMAS STOPPED TO pick up a dozen roses for Rebecca and a bottle of wine, hoping to mellow Rebecca for their talk. He should have told her sooner about the job offer.

He just prayed she'd understand.

And that she'd consider coming with him.

If she didn't...could he stay in Sugar Hill? Live in the small town and practice medicine?

All the pros and cons warred with one another in his head as he drove through the small town. The friends he'd made, the warmth of the people, the content feeling that engulfed him when he saw his patients with their new babies, the safe streets and countryside which would be perfect for family life.

But the negatives echoed just as well—the lack of specialists, the distance for emergencies, the limitations of the hospital. His vow to his parents and the little baby brother he'd lost....

In Atlanta he could afford a big house with a yard, and could give his child the best of everything. He and Rebecca could move into a nice neighborhood in the suburbs with a pool and tennis courts, and Rebecca could show her paintings. They could have it all. With her love of books and art, she would make a great conversationalist at parties. Plus, her volunteer work at the church and that reading club she'd started with the kids at her bookstore could filter over to PTA events and their own family. And her experience as a small-business owner would bring practical advice to any committee she might want to chair.

If she chose not to serve on any of them or help with fund-raisers, hell, he could hire an assistant to take care of those things.

Determined he'd ironed out the details for a smooth transition for both of them, he parked his car, grabbed the flowers and wine and hurried up the steps. He knocked and waited, his heart pounding.

He was so excited over his upcoming plans; Rebecca just had to agree. Surely she wouldn't think he was rushing things.

But she had told her grandmother she wasn't getting married. Only, that was before they'd gotten involved. Before she'd stolen his heart and he'd taken her virginity.

Still, his hands shook as he pushed the doorbell again, and his pulse clamored like a teenager's asking for his first date.

Would Rebecca be shocked when he admitted he loved her? And what would she say to his proposal?

Chapter Eighteen

Rebecca had just packed away the erotic poetry book, the bride's book and garter and closed the hope chest, shutting out her dreams of marriage and babies, when the doorbell rang. Ten o'clock—who would be visiting her now?

Thomas? No, he was probably spending the night in Atlanta. Her father's dinner parties usually ran late, and there were always drinks flowing and laughter and lots of business acquaintances. Plus it had started to rain, creating hazardous traffic conditions. She'd been listening to it pound the roof for hours.

The chime sounded again, and she pulled her bathrobe around her and forced her legs to move, when all she really wanted to do was collapse on the bed with a good book and have another cry.

It was probably Gertrude and Jerry with more talk about their wedding plans. She'd paste on a cheery face and be happy for them if it killed her.

But she opened the door and saw Thomas on the other side, rain sluicing off him. His handsome face and smile sent a thunderous roar of pain through her.

"Can I come in?" His hand snaked from behind his back to reveal a bouquet of roses. "I missed you."

Tears seemed to choke her throat, but she swallowed and accepted the flowers, then moved aside. "They're beautiful."

She walked to the kitchen, grabbed a vase and put the flowers in water, clipping the stems carefully, stalling as long as possible. At least until she could string together a coherent sentence. He flipped the kitchen towel off the counter and swiped at his damp hair and clothes. She itched to take the towel and dry his face but gripped the vase, resisting.

Finally she turned to him, unease rippling through her at the odd way he was staring at her. But she sucked up her courage, determined not to make a dramatic scene. She should have just told him goodbye the night of Grammy's party when she'd overheard his conversation with her dad.

"We have to talk, Rebecca."

Here it comes. The flowers were obviously his way of easing into his breakup speech.

He moved inside the kitchen, found the corkscrew she kept in the drawer as if he was right at home, then opened the wine he'd brought and poured them each a glass.

Wine to soften the blow….

Then he handed her one glass and gathered her free hand in his and led her to the sofa. His dark eyes gleamed with emotions she didn't understand as he raked them over her. Then he urged her down beside him. "I…I should have mentioned this before, but…" He took a sip of his wine, suddenly looking nervous, so she sipped hers, then he set his glass down, took hers from her, and pulled both her hands in his. She'd never seen him so nervous. ''I went to Atlanta today. I wanted to talk to the board of the new women's medical center being set up there about working with them. Have you heard of it?''

Rebecca nodded. She had to be brave. ''I've heard my father mention it.'' *Just like I heard you talk to him before you left.*

''Of course.'' He squeezed her hands, studying them for a few minutes, and Rebecca's heart melted. This would be the last time she would hold his hand. Touch him.

''I met your father, the other directors of the board and some of the physicians. It's a remarkable facility and the possibilities for advanced-medicine techniques are amazing.''

''I know, Dad's very excited.''

''Anyway, I just don't see the same opportunities for me here in Sugar Hill.''

Yeah, like more sophisticated women. ''So you already accepted the job?''

He nodded. ''I'm going to talk to Hannah about bringing another doctor onboard immediately. Meanwhile I'll come back once a week to see my patients or, if they choose, they can drive to Atlanta. Otherwise, Dr. Taylor in the next county will take on some patients, those Hannah might not be able to handle.''

Rebecca pulled her hand from his. ''I hope you'll be happy there.''

His smile faded slightly, his forehead creasing. ''It's everything I've ever wanted, Rebecca. I have to take this opportunity, but I want—''

"You used me to get to know my father so you could get this job."

His mouth gaped but guilt flashed into his eyes. "What?"

"I heard you at my grandmother's party, Thomas. I knew you were going to talk to my father today."

He ran a hand over the rough stubble of his beard, looking panic-stricken.

"You didn't have to sleep with me or bring me flowers or wine. You could have simply asked, and I would have introduced you." She waved her hand around, fighting emotions. "Romancing me wasn't necessary."

He jerked up. "Geez, Rebecca, just listen, I didn't—"

"You didn't date me so you could meet my dad? Come on, Thomas." Anger tinged her voice now. "Once I heard you at the party, I put two and two together. I must admit you flattered me at first, but the timing should have been obvious, the way you showed up at the café at the same time my father did that day, the way you finagled an invitation to Grammy's party, you even complimented my paintings—"

"I complimented your art because I liked it. You're very talented, Rebecca, but you hide your talent away here in this small town."

"I like this small town. I'm happy here." She folded her arms. "But you charmed me, and you're good at it, Thomas. Better than I would have imagined, but maybe that's because I was such an innocent little fool."

"No." He grabbed her arms and forced her to face him. "I admit that at first I wanted you to introduce me to Bert, but then I got to know you and I fell in love with you—''

Hurt knifed through her again. ''It's over, Thomas, you don't have to keep up this act—''

''It's not an act.'' His dark eyes flared. ''I came here to tell you I love you, and to ask you to move to Atlanta with me.''

She stared at him, the emotions in his eyes confusing her even more. ''To come with you?''

''Yes, we can get married and buy a big house in the city or the suburbs and you can show your art there. You won't have to work at the bookstore. I can support us so you can open a studio if you want and you'll be fantastic with the committees—''

''I like running the bookstore,'' she said, unable to believe how little he understood her. He was more like her father than she'd ever imagined. He had the drive, the ambition, the intelligence, and he wanted the wife to help him make it to the top.

But she could never be what he wanted, what her father had wanted her to be all these years. And she would not make herself miserable trying.

''I'm not moving from Sugar Hill, Thomas. I finally have a home.''

''Why not?'' Thomas shook her gently. ''We can have it all in Atlanta.''

''Don't you understand? I have it all here.'' *At least I thought I did.* ''I've never approved of my father's trophy wives, and I certainly don't fit the image.''

''I want *you,* Rebecca, not some trophy wife.''

''Do you, Thomas?'' She stared at him long and hard. ''Or do you want that sophisticated woman who'll raise money for the center, who'll hobnob with the rich and famous and be the perfect doctor's wife?''

His throat worked as he swallowed.

''Because I like small-town life. I like owning my own business and working with the children at story hour. I like painting for myself and my family. I don't need to be rich or famous like you do.''

''For God's sake, Rebecca, this is not about me wanting to be rich or famous. It's about helping people.''

''Then why do you have to leave? You have a great job here. The people in Sugar Hill respect and love you. They need you just as much as the people in Atlanta, maybe more, because we don't have all the choices of medical care. So if this is about helping people or loving me, you wouldn't need to move.''

His heart raced painfully in his chest. He was losing her; he could feel it.

When he spoke, his voice was low, full of hurt. ''If you cared about me, you wouldn't mind moving, Rebecca.'' His voice turned gravelly, breaking. ''But you obviously don't love me.'' He paced across the room, ran his hand through his hair, stood at the window for several seconds, then turned, and his gaze fell to the desk in the corner. To the books on pregnancy she'd bought months before. His gaze rose to meet hers, and pain and suspicion flashed in the dark depths. ''Are you pregnant?''

''No.''

A muscle ticked in his jaw. ''Don't lie to me, Rebecca.''

''I'm not. I swear I'm not pregnant, Thomas. I would never lie about that.''

"But you wanted to be?"

She couldn't very well deny it, so she nodded. "It...it all started with that hope chest."

A puzzled look crossed his face. Then suddenly the hurt in his eyes flared into anger. "That e-mail—you sent away for information for yourself. You lied to me."

The devastation in his voice was so raw that she realized she had to make him understand. "Thomas, it's not how it looks."

"You accused me of dating you to get to know your father, but you used me, too, didn't you? You wanted a baby, and I gave you the perfect reason not to go to a sperm clinic. I was the real thing." He stepped backward toward the door, his face pale. "That's the reason you showed up at my door and seduced me."

"No, at first I wanted to ask you, but I was so shy..." She clenched her hands into fists, dug her fingernails into her palms. It was time to end this before they hurt each other any more. "I thought you...you would never love me. I wanted to ask you to help me, but then..."

"Then what, Rebecca?"

"Then..." How could she admit she loved him when he still didn't want her for herself? When they wanted such different things in life. "Then...we sort of got involved."

He dropped his gaze from her face then, the seed of hope she'd seen sprout for a moment washing away with anger and betrayal. Then he shook his head and turned and walked out the door.

Rebecca felt her heart being ripped out.

But she didn't move, because she had no idea how

to fix what had gone wrong, so she let him take her bleeding heart with him.

HURT, BETRAYAL AND ANGER bombarded Thomas as he drove to his house. Rebecca has used him just as his mother had used his father. And when he'd found that stupid e-mail and confronted her, she'd lied to him, and he had believed her.

If she'd gotten pregnant, would she have sent him out of her life as his mother had his dad?

Emotions tightened his chest as he let himself inside the house. The empty walls screeched with silence, yet everywhere he looked and turned, he sensed Rebecca. Her perfume lingered in the den, the sight of her wearing his shirt while she made coffee in the kitchen as vivid as it had been the morning after she'd spent her first night with him. And the imprint of their bodies lying together on the pillows in front of the fireplace would be etched in his mind forever.

He'd been a fool.

He tossed his jacket onto the cold leather sofa and picked up the phone to call Trish Tieney, his Realtor. He'd tell her to put the house on the market tomorrow.

Then he'd call Hannah and work out some kind of arrangement for his patients so he could start the job in Atlanta as soon as possible.

There was nothing left for him in Sugar Hill.

Maybe there never had been.

Chapter Nineteen

The next day Rebecca phoned in sick. Business had slowed with the new year, and Gertrude could handle any customers that did drop in. Besides, she couldn't face the possibility of running into Thomas downtown.

It wasn't likely, she reminded herself. In fact, he would probably be avoiding her.

Fueled with hurt and anger and running on nerves, she spent the day cleaning out closets, reorganizing her bookshelves and trying to forget him.

But echoes of his voice remained in her small apartment, remnants of his compliments and tender touches and lovemaking whispered to her at the oddest moments. Like when she'd smelled his cologne on one of her new shirts. And when she'd gathered items for the cleaners and remembered the way he'd looked at her in that violet dress.

And her art—she'd avoided painting, even going into her studio because Thomas's face flashed into her head each time she looked at an empty canvas. She'd been so nervous about allowing him to see her art, yet he'd immediately alleviated her anxiety by praising her work.

Had everything been a lie?

The doorbell chimed and she froze, half wanting it to be Thomas, but knowing it wouldn't be. Probably Jerry. She wasn't in the mood to hear about his new-found love.

It chimed incessantly, though, so she finally dragged herself to the door. Instead of Jerry, her cousins Hannah, Mimi and Alison stood on the stoop with bags of ice cream in their hands and sympathy in their eyes.

"Thomas called and told me he's moving," Hannah said softly.

"I'm so sorry," Alison whispered.

Mimi looked furious. "He's a dirtbag. But don't worry, Bec, we'll find you someone better."

Rebecca's lip trembled. "That's just it…I don't want anyone else. I—love him."

"Ahh, sugar," her cousins murmured.

They pulled her into a group hug, and she tried to make herself believe everything would be all right. But she didn't think she would ever survive losing Thomas.

And she didn't know how she'd get over loving him.

THOMAS WAS MISERABLE all week.

Hannah had offered to take over his patients and had relieved him immediately.

Apparently she wanted him out of Sugar Hill as fast as possible.

Just as Rebecca obviously did. Until the last second, he'd hoped she would stop by to see him and tell him their whole nightmarish conversation had been a figment of his imagination.

But that hadn't happened. And it wouldn't. He was too much of a realist to expect miracles.

So, he'd checked into a rental suite at a hotel in Atlanta until he could find time to house shop. He had already moved into his office and would start seeing patients next week. This week had been filled with committee meetings, routine sessions on acclimatizing himself to the new facility and their philosophy, along with all the accompanying red tape—he'd forgotten all the politics and paperwork attached to a bureaucracy.

He opened a box of medical journals and began to stack them on the polished cherry bookshelves in his plush new office. He'd have plenty of time to keep up with journals now that his weekends wouldn't be tied up with a woman or a family.

Every good doctor had to make sacrifices.

He glanced around at the pristine walls, looked out the windows at the impressive view of the city and smiled. He had achieved his goals.

So, why did he feel so empty inside?

It wasn't as if Rebecca missed him or wanted him back in her life.

A knock on his door jerked him from his thoughts. Before he could even reply, Suzanne Hartwell flounced in and stalked toward his desk, brandishing a bad attitude that he didn't quite understand.

"You scum bucket, how dare you hurt my sister like you did!" She pointed a sharp, blood-red fingernail at him that looked lethal. "I can't believe you used her to get to know Daddy. Buddy, if I'd known your intentions, I would have told him not to hire you!"

"Is that what Rebecca told you?" he asked, irked by her attitude. After all, Rebecca had used him, too.

Not that it alleviated his own guilt.

"No, she hasn't told me anything, but Mimi called, and I talked to Hannah and Alison."

"Oh, dear God, is your uncle Wiley running our personal lives on a billboard now?"

"Don't you dare insult my family," Suzanne stammered. "I have a good mind to tell Daddy what you did—"

"Then tell him how his lovely daughter used me because she wanted a baby."

"What?" Suzanne barked out a laugh. "That's the most ridiculous thing I've ever heard."

"But it's true." He stood and gripped the desk with white-knuckled fists, then leaned forward, pushing his face in her angry one. "I went to her to propose and—"

"You proposed?"

"Yes, but—" he waved off her obvious surprise "—but she turned me down."

"She turned you down?"

"Yes," he ground out. "It seems the only thing she wanted out of me was a baby."

"I don't believe you." Her voice rose in indignation. "Rebecca wouldn't use anybody."

Suzanne had left the door wide open, and Bert strode in, arms waving. "What the hell is going on in here? I heard you two shouting all the way down the hall."

Suzanne aimed a warning look at Thomas. "He hurt Rebecca."

"What?" Bert staggered back and grabbed the door. "Is she okay?"

"No, she's so brokenhearted she can't even paint." Suzanne gave Thomas a furious look. "And now he's accusing her of using him, when it was the other way around."

"I asked her to marry me," Thomas argued when Bert lunged forward. "I wanted her to move here with me, but she refused."

Bert froze, his body wobbling as he sank into a nearby leather chair. Suzanne made a clicking sound with her mouth.

"Why did you ask her to move here?" Suzanne asked.

Insanity clutched at Thomas. Didn't these people understand English? "Because I love her, why else?"

Bert's mouth flopped open, then closed. "Is she in love with you?"

"Yes," Suzanne said.

"No," Thomas said at the same time.

Bert glanced from one to the other, obviously perplexed. "I don't understand what's going on here at all."

Thomas was losing patience with them both. "Maybe that's because you haven't paid very much attention to Rebecca lately," Thomas said. "Or maybe you never did."

Bert's head snapped up. "What's that supposed to mean, young man?"

"It means you ignore her," Thomas said, knowing he'd probably lose his job, but for once he didn't care. He had to speak his mind. "You dote on Suzanne but you hardly even speak to Rebecca when she's around. It's so obvious it's pathetic. Maybe Rebecca is shy, but there's nothing wrong with that, and it certainly doesn't mean she's not as intelligent or beautiful."

Suzanne was watching him with a strange look on her face. He realized he was babbling so he clamped his mouth shut.

"I...that's not true." Bert dropped his head forward into chubby hands, emotions overcoming him. "Could Wiley be right?"

Thomas inhaled sharply, confused now himself. Suzanne twisted her hands in front of her as if she was at a loss, too.

"I do love Rebecca," Bert finally choked out. "It's just..."

Suzanne edged toward her father and placed a hand on his shoulder. When he sobbed out loud, she stooped down and patted him. "It's what, Dad?"'

Bert raised his head and glanced up at her, then at Thomas, tears brimming in his eyes. "It's just that she reminds me so much of your mother." A tear rolled down his ruddy cheek into his beard. "I was so lost when your mother died, and Rebecca, she...every time I looked at her, I saw your mother. It hurt so much sometimes I could barely breathe."

Thomas swallowed, shocked at the man's confession. Did Rebecca have any idea how he felt? She had probably been vying for her father's love all her life.

Just as he had his own father. Had he thought becoming more successful would bring his own father back into his life?

Bert dragged out a handkerchief and wiped at his eyes. "Rebecca and your mama were so close. They were both quiet. They liked art and books and then when I..." He gripped his hands into knots. "When we couldn't save your mama from cancer, Rebecca withdrew and I didn't know how to help her. How to reach her." He had his hand on top of Suzanne's.

"You were easy, you cried and let it all out, but Rebecca, she felt everything so deep, just like your mother."

Thomas sympathized with Bert. Every family reacted to grief in their own way, and sometimes they let each other down in the process of recovery. "Dr. Hartwell." Thomas cleared his throat. "With all due respect, I think you're telling the wrong people here."

"Huh?" He sniffed, dragged out a monogrammed handkerchief and blew his nose.

"You need to tell Rebecca," Thomas said in a low voice. "She needs to hear this, not us."

Bert's questioning gaze lasted a half second, then he nodded. "You're right, son. It's time I fix my relationship with my daughter."

Suzanne hugged her father, then turned to Thomas. "Now, what about you? Are you going to fix your relationship with my sister?"

THE DAY AFTER HER COUSINS left, Rebecca drove up to Pine Mountain to see her grandmother. She'd thought the fresh country air and beautiful scenery would help her regain perspective. She'd even brought her paints and a new canvas, but they sat untouched in her car.

She kept remembering the last time she'd been here. The day Grammy had given her the hope chest and she'd smashed into Thomas's car.

The day their romance had begun. It seemed like years ago.

"But now it's over, Grammy," Rebecca said, hating the telltale quaver of her voice.

Grammy plunked down beside her in the glider on the screened-in front porch. The winter wind whistled softly through the mountain, the dried leaves and bare trees mirroring Rebecca's empty, aching heart.

Grammy quirked a gray brow. "You say he proposed to you, child, but he wanted you to be different?"

Rebecca searched her memory for Thomas's exact words. "Well, not exactly. But he's ambitious like Daddy and works with him and—"

"And you think just because your father has these pretty wives on his arm that your young man is just like him."

"He's not my young man," Rebecca said.

"He can be if you want him."

"But I do." Didn't Grammy understand a single word she'd been saying?

Grammy wrapped Rebecca's hands into her age-spotted ones. "Do you know why I think your father keeps marrying these showy women?"

Rebecca shook her head.

"Because they are the exact opposite of your mother, dear."

Rebecca frowned.

"I believe your daddy loved your mama so much that he never got over her. Him being a doctor and all, he just couldn't get past the guilt of not being able to save her."

"But the doctors did everything possible, didn't they?"

"Yes, of course. Emotions aren't always rational, you know."

Hers certainly hadn't been lately, not since the day she'd received her hope chest and slammed into Thomas's car.

Grammy pursed her lips. "Sometimes doctors, especially men, think they're supposed to save the entire world. And when they can't save someone they love, they become more driven."

Rebecca remembered the pain in Thomas's voice when he'd confided about his brother. Her father and Thomas were so much alike....

"But your father's marriages haven't lasted, because they're not built on love. They're filled with empty hopes and business functions and then he soon realizes that, and the woman gets the money she wants and they split up."

"How sad for Daddy," Rebecca said, really considering the extent of his devastation over her mother's loss for the first time since she was little. And then he'd been left with two daughters to raise alone.

"Now, if your young man is as wonderful as you say he is, I have a feeling he meant it when he confessed his love."

Rebecca's heart gave a funny little flutter.

"Don't let pride, or the fact that you've always been shy, stop you from going after what you want, Rebecca." Grammy made a tsking sound. "Sometimes you have to take a chance and put your heart out there."

"But I did that and look what happened. He wanted me to be someone else."

"Did he?" Grammy's eyes sparkled with wisdom. "Or did he see something wonderful in you that you may not have realized? You know, the best mates are the ones who challenge us to be all we can be. That may take us out of our comfort zone, but it's because they love us that they see under the surface. That means they understood our fears, too, but they have confidence we can overcome them." She patted Rebecca's hand. "Just remember," she said in a low voice, "true love comes around once in a lifetime. Isn't it worth making a few sacrifices for?"

Rebecca hugged her grandmother, analyzing their conversation as she started back to Sugar Hill. Could she sacrifice the life she'd built in Sugar Hill, her family and friends and her work for the chance of a new life with Thomas?

And if she could, would he even want her after what he believed she'd done?

BEFORE THOMAS COULD REPLY to Suzanne's question or decide how to make things right with Rebecca, his receptionist tapped on the door. "Excuse me, Dr. Emerson, but you had a phone call from your old office in Sugar Hill. Dr. Tippins thought you'd want to know that a Mr. Lackey called."

"Yes?"

"The Lackey baby had to have emergency surgery. She figured you'd want to be there."

Panic seized him. After all the couple and that infant had endured, they had to face another surgery, more waiting. He gave Suzanne and Bert an apologetic look. "I have to go. We'll finish this talk later."

Suzanne frowned but Bert nodded, and Thomas rushed out the door. They couldn't lose the Lackey baby now, they just couldn't.

Chapter Twenty

The next three hours were excruciating. Thomas sat with the Lackeys, offering them reassurances when he had no idea what the outcome for their baby would be. Not being involved in the surgery himself gave him an entirely different perspective on the case and the emotions the parents faced while waiting. It also resurrected those old haunting memories of losing his baby brother and feeling helpless.

The only thing they could do was pray.

It humbled him to realize that Rebecca was right. Although the surgeon had excellent credentials, no one could predict the future—no one except God.

He watched the Lackeys cling to each other and turn to their faith, and he prayed along with them, the minutes on the clock ticking by as if in slow motion. When the surgeon finally appeared in the doorway, he had to steady Mr. Lackey as he stood to greet the other doctor.

"The baby is fine," Dr. Lowenbrau said in a thick New York accent. "The surgery was a complete success. Barring fever or complications, you should be able to take your son home with you in a few days."

The Lackeys hugged and whooped with joy, both crying deliriously.

Lowenbrau shook Thomas's hand. "It's a good thing that couple had you on their side when the baby was born. You saved that little boy's life by getting him to us so quickly."

Thomas nodded, although he knew the Lackeys didn't share that sentiment. He even understood their frustration and their need to blame.

But Mr. Lackey turned to him and swiped at tears. "Doc, I owe you an apology."

Thomas waved it away with a hand. "That's not necessary."

Mr. Lackey cleared his throat. "Yes, it is. I said some harsh words right after little Tyler was born. I was hurt and angry and I lashed out at you. I…I've been ashamed ever since."

Thomas's throat closed.

"My wife and I, well, we appreciate you taking care of our son that day, and coming to us now." Mrs. Lackey dried her tears on her husband's handkerchief. "Most doctors wouldn't take the time to do what you've done for us, to sit here and wait with us."

"You've been more than a doctor, you've been a friend." She threw her arms around him and hugged him.

Moisture pricked Thomas's eyes. He'd been searching for recognition and love in his career, and his job had brought him to the town that could give him both.

And to the woman who could give him the love he had always needed so much.

Rebecca claimed that Sugar Hill needed him more than the people in the city did, and she was right. He needed them, too. But he'd already turned in his resignation. Had Hannah replaced him?

Worse, was it too late for him and Rebecca—had she only wanted him for the purpose of making a baby? Had she loved him at all? He had to believe she had, that she couldn't have given herself to him if she didn't have feelings for him. But he'd deceived her....

Had he lost her forever?

REBECCA HAD MEANT to drive home to Sugar Hill from her grandmother's, but her old jalopy had a mind of its own. Or maybe it just knew her heart lay with a man in the city so it had raced there on autopilot.

Anyway, she had no idea where Thomas was staying or if he would even talk to her, but the only way to find out was to ask her father.

She dreaded seeing him.

Her legs wobbled as she took the elevator to her father's office. He would probably demand to know why she wanted to see Thomas. Hopefully, she'd be able to explain without completely falling apart. But she would not lie again. Not to her father or to Thomas or even to herself.

When she'd given her wardrobe and face a makeover and become a new bolder woman, she'd only taken baby steps. Now she had to take a bigger one, dig deeper into her soul, forget the safety net she clung to....

Sucking in a deep breath, she opened the door to her father's receptionist's office. An attractive woman in her midfifties peered over bifocals. "Yes?"

"I'm Rebecca Hartwell. I came to see my father. Is he in?"

"Yes, as a matter of fact, he's been trying to call you, dear. Go on in."

He'd been trying to call her? Was something wrong? Suzanne...

Panic seized her chest as she knocked on her father's door. She didn't wait for him to answer. "Dad?"

His face lit with surprise, then he rose and crossed the room in quick strides and wrapped her in a hug. "I've been calling you for an hour. God, I'm glad you're here, baby."

"What's wrong?" She angled her head back enough to study his face. His eyes looked slightly red and his voice was hoarse. Had her father been crying?

Oh, heavens, it *was* Suzanne, that would be the only thing that would upset him so much.

Her knees felt weak. She had to sit down. Trembling, she practically dragged him along to the leather love seat in the sitting area.

"Dad, what's happened? Is Suzanne all right?"

"Suzanne?" His eyebrows drew together in a frown. "Suzanne's fine as far as I know. Why? Did you hear something?" Now he looked panicked.

"No, no, but you look upset. I figured it had to be Suzanne. And your receptionist said you've been calling me and you never call..." She let the sentence trail off when she saw tears pool in his eyes again. "Dad, what's happened? You're scaring me."

He sniffled, then shook his head. "I'm sorry, darling, I...I..."

He'd called her "darling"? He hadn't done that since grade school. "You what, Dad?"

Yanking out a handkerchief, he wiped at perspiration popping out on his forehead. "I've been a terrible father to you. I...I didn't mean to be, I really didn't. I'm just an old fool."

Rebecca sank back against the cool leather, stunned.

"You're right, I never call, but that's going to change. I realize it seems like I've favored Suzanne, but that's not true."

Rebecca clung to the edge of the love seat, the pain she'd felt over the years shifting slightly at the emotions thickening his voice.

He dropped his head forward, then jerked it up and looked at her, really stared at her face, something he hadn't done in so long. "I'm not excusing myself, but you have to know the reason. It's not that I love her more, it's just...just that when I lost your mother, I was so devastated." He sucked in a harsh breath.

"I didn't know how to go on without her. She was so quiet, and everyone thought she depended on me, but it was the other way around. She was my backbone. My...my everything."

Rebecca's heart stammered, missing a beat.

"Then she was gone and I felt guilty. Guilty that I couldn't save her." He rolled his fingers out and stared at them, flexing them and studying the tips. "After all that medical training, I couldn't save the most important person in my life."

"Oh, Dad." Rebecca cradled an arm around his neck. "You're not God. You did everything you could."

"I knew that up here," he said, pointing to his head. "But I couldn't accept it. Then I had you and Suzanne to face." He brushed a knuckle across her cheek. "You were so devastated, and withdrew into your books and art. I didn't know how to reach you. Your mother always knew how to do that, though. She was my rock."

"But I needed you," Rebecca whispered, for the first time in her life admitting how much his withdrawal had cost her.

"I know, and I'm sorry. It's just that you look so much like your mother." His voice turned huskier as if it hurt to say the words out loud. "I ached to look at you. Every time I did, I saw her and felt the loss all over again. All the guilt would rush back."

"I'm so sorry, Dad," Rebecca whispered, near choking. "I didn't understand."

"I poured myself into work to ease the pain. I kept thinking if I knew more, if I learned more about medicine, I'd never lose anyone else that I loved." A tear slid down his cheek. "But in doing so I lost you. You slipped farther and farther away and I didn't know how to cope." He cleared his throat. "You are so beautiful, Rebecca. So quiet and sensitive and intuitive, just like she was." He paused, collected himself again and squeezed her hand in his. "She could paint, too, you know. I still have the painting she gave me for our first anniversary."

For the first time in ages, Rebecca realized how much her father had truly loved her mother. And why he'd chosen such opposite types to marry since then. Grammy was right. He'd never been able to replace the love of his life.

Another reason she couldn't lose hers.

She hugged him fiercely. "I love you, Dad."

"I love you, too, and I promise, sweetheart, if you

give me another chance, things will be better. I'd do anything for you.''

Rebecca nodded, wiping at her own tears. ''Then I have a favor to ask.''

''Anything, just name it.''

''Do you know where Thomas is staying? I...I need to talk to him.''

His eyebrow rose, and she braced herself for the onslaught of questions. Instead he stood and grabbed a pad, then scribbled an address. ''He's at this hotel. But he's probably not there right now.''

Disappointment flitted through her.

''Hannah called about the Lackey baby he delivered in Sugar Hill. The doctors in Atlanta had to do emergency surgery.''

''Oh, no. Is the baby okay?''

Her father shrugged. ''I haven't heard yet. Thomas tore out of here to sit with the Lackeys. You should find him at the hospital.''

Rebecca hugged her father one last time. Thomas cared so much about that infant, he would be worried sick. She needed to be with him, to show him that she cared, too. That she understood the reason he was so driven, and that she would always be there for him to lean on. That she would be his rock.

She'd hidden inside her baggy dresses and the safety of the small town and her family long enough. She would let him know that whatever he decided to do, she would stand beside him.

That is, if he still wanted her....

She raced out the door, then practically ran to her car. But when she jumped inside and turned the key, the darned jalopy wouldn't start. She banged the steering wheel and tried again.

This could not be happening....

WHEN THOMAS LEFT the hospital, he drove straight to the florist's shop. He didn't want to arrive at Rebecca's without some kind of flower in hand. A few minutes later he'd made his selection, then swung back by his office to pick up his briefcase and cell phone. He jogged up the steps, hurriedly grabbed his things and took the elevator down, tapping his foot impatiently. What if he was too late? What if Rebecca didn't believe him?

What if she really didn't love him?

His head ached with worry as he found his Porsche in the dark garage. He shoved his briefcase to the floor, turned the key, then put the car in reverse. Now that he'd decided to talk to Rebecca, he couldn't wait. He had to see her tonight. He checked his watch. By the time he arrived it would be midnight. He needed to hurry.

Tension knotted his muscles and neck as he cranked the car. Distracted by his thoughts, he threw the gearshift into reverse and rammed the gas. He glanced back just in time to see a car careening down the aisle, but he didn't hit the brakes fast enough and he slammed into it. Metal crunched, the tires of the other car squealed, and the car spun and slammed into the concrete boulder support in the middle of the parking lot.

Damn.

He threw his door open and gasped in horror at the twisted, mangled heap of metal. He recognized the clunker station wagon immediately. It belonged to Rebecca.

Chapter Twenty-One

Oh, dear heavens, not again.

Rebecca's entire body quivered with the shock of the impact. Then suddenly Thomas appeared at her door, pulling her out and checking her over, and she was too stunned to speak.

"Rebecca, are you okay?" He gripped her arms gently. "Tell me, are you hurt anywhere? Did you hit your head?"

She shook her head. "I'm s-sorry."

"Dammit, it wasn't your fault this time. It was mine. Now answer me, are you hurt?"

"No. I'm fine."

A harsh breath escaped him, then he dragged her into his arms. "You scared the hell out of me."

She clung to him until her shaking subsided, but unfortunately a different sort of trembling began deep inside, a trembling spurred by desire and fear and hope.

But she didn't come here to cling to him or get sympathy; she came to prove she was strong and independent. That she was ready to take a chance.

She slowly extricated herself from his embrace, and

he straightened his sportscoat, squaring his broad shoulders. "I'll pay for the damages," he said stiffly.

"Forget the car," Rebecca said, remembering his words the day she'd hit him at her grandmother's house.

His eyebrows shot up. "But it's probably totaled."

"I said forget the damn car."

Surprise registered, then a half smile played on his lips. "So...what were you doing here, anyway?"

"I came to see you. I...I heard about the Lackey baby."

"Oh." His smile faded.

"Is he going to be okay?"

"The prognosis is good. He survived surgery with flying colors and should be able to go home soon." He ran a hand over his face, drawing her gaze to the thick five-o'clock shadow. The stubble that had scraped her skin when he'd kissed her. She wanted it to touch her again. But Thomas wasn't moving toward her, and she was losing her nerve.

"Is that the only reason you came?"

"No." She gestured toward the building.

"You came to visit your father?"

Was that disappointment lacing his voice. "I...yes, I saw him."

"You've been crying," he said in a gruff voice. His hand reached out tentatively to brush her cheek. "Did he hurt you?"

"No," she said, emotions pulling at her. "Everything's fine."

He nodded. The silence stretching between them was so painful Rebecca closed her eyes and willed herself courage. When she opened them, Thomas was watching her with a mixture of wariness and some other emotion she couldn't quite read.

It was now or never.

"Actually, I came for another reason."

He waited, his eyes flickering with a moment of hunger. At least she hoped it was hunger.

"I'm moving to Atlanta."

This time shock registered on his face. "You're moving here?" He turned and glanced inside her car, then back at her, a puzzled look in his eyes. "But you didn't bring anything with you."

She licked her lips, then shrugged. "Th-that's," she paused and focused so she wouldn't stutter, then reached out and took his hand. "That's because everything I need is already here. In fact, it's standing right in front of me."

Thomas's lips parted slightly as if he was going to reply, his breath wheezing out, then he squeezed her hand.

Hope fluttered inside her. "I don't know if you still want me or not, Thomas, but I had to come and tell you how I feel."

"And how do you feel, Rebecca?" he asked in a throaty voice.

"I love you." She slowly dropped to her knees, then pulled their joined hands to her lips and kissed his palm. "I love you and I need you and I want to be there for you, Thomas." She hesitated, her voice shaking, but continued, "You asked me once to marry you and move to Atlanta with you. I want that, Thomas. If you still want me."

His dark eyes raked over her, his long look so tension-filled that her courage weakened. He swallowed, then slowly released her hand and left her. His footsteps echoed on the hard pavement, pounding in the fact that he had turned her down. Then he opened the car door and her heart stopped as she waited. Was he leaving? Going to drive away with her stooped on bended knee?

Humiliation stung Rebecca's cheeks, the emptiness inside her so agonizing she nearly curled into a ball on the cold pavement. Instead, she stared at her banged-up car, wondering if she had the strength to crawl to it.

THOMAS REACHED INSIDE the Porsche, picked up the flowers he'd bought and turned to Rebecca, his heart in his throat. Her confession had shocked him so much he hadn't been able to speak. Rebecca was willing to move to Atlanta to be with him....

He gripped the flowers in a shaky hand, then circled back and stood in front of her. "Actually, I was leaving in such a hurry because I was on my way back to see you."

"You were?" Her gaze rose, the tears that glittered in those eyes tearing at him.

"Yes. I wanted to give you these." He offered her the arrangement and watched as she examined the rose-colored heart-shaped pendant flowers. She lifted the flowers to her nose and sniffed. "Its technical term is *dicentra formosa....*"

Her gaze locked with his. "Yes."

"Otherwise known as a—"

"Bleeding heart."

"My bleeding heart." His love for her was so intense he felt raw inside. "I was coming back to Sugar

Hill to give it to you. To ask you to forgive me and heal my wounded heart.'' Moisture clogged his throat as he knelt in front of her. ''I love you, Rebecca. Without you my life is empty. I'm so sorry I hurt you—''

She pressed a finger to his lips. ''We both hurt each other. But that's in the past.''

''That means we have a future?''

She nodded. ''If you want one with me.''

''I don't want one without you. I need you, Rebecca, I love you with all my heart.'' His dark eyes turned almost black with hunger. ''But there's one problem.''

''What?'' she asked softly.

''We have to live in Sugar Hill.''

''No, I was wrong not to compromise,'' she said. ''It doesn't matter where we live as long as we're together.''

''You're right about that, sweetheart. Just like you were right about me—about the reason I pushed myself and about the town needing me.'' He brought her fingers to his lips and kissed them. ''But I still want to live in Sugar Hill. Everything I want is there.'' He pressed a hand to her stomach. ''Of course, I'm open if some little people want to join us in the future.''

Then he took her in his arms and sealed his love with a kiss. Passion rocked through him, the tenderness in her touch so humbling that the empty void he'd felt in his life for so long suddenly overflowed with the promise of tomorrow.

''Uh, er, excuse me.'' A deep, throaty voice broke into the kiss.

Thomas glanced up to see a beefy security guard

leaning over the edge of the dented Porsche, hands on his chunky hips. "You two okay?"

Rebecca giggled and he nodded. "Yes, sir, we're fine."

He shone his flashlight at them, then toward the dented cars blocking the exit of the parking lot. "These your cars?"

"Yes, sir."

"Had an accident, huh?"

Thomas helped Rebecca stand. "No, sir, I believe it was serendipity."

The cop scratched his head, looking puzzled. "Need to file insurance papers or something?"

"No." Thomas circled his arm around Rebecca. "The only paper we're going to file is a marriage certificate."

LATER, AS THEY LAY in the king-size bed in Thomas's hotel room, sated and cuddled up in each other's arms, Rebecca pressed tender kisses along his jaw. On the way to the hotel, she had murmured one of the erotic love poems to him, and their passion had exploded. Now she gazed at her husband-to-be in awe. How could she ever have been afraid to take a chance on love when her heart had known all along that Thomas was the man for her?

"No more secrets between us, no more lies," Thomas whispered.

"No," Rebecca said against his chest. "Not ever."

But Thomas's phone rang, jarring them from their blissful moment. He stared at it once, then frowned. Rebecca angled her head to look up at him and traced a finger along his hairline.

"Go ahead," she whispered. "It might be an emergency."

He nodded. "Dr. Emerson." Seconds later he angled his head toward her and covered the speaker with his hand, a wary look darkening his eyes. "It's this art dealer from midtown. I forgot to tell you that I took him one of your art pieces. I wanted to surprise you."

She sat up, jerking the sheet to her. Dear heavens, she'd forgotten the painting.

He mouthed, "I'm sorry," then turned back to the phone. "You have what? A buyer for both paintings. What second painting?" His eyes suddenly widened. "A painting of two nude lovers on a mountainside?"

His gaze swung to hers, his eyebrow arched as he pointed to his chest in question.

Rebecca nodded.

"Don't sell it," Thomas screeched. "I'm buying both pieces. We'll stop by to pick them up tomorrow."

He hung up, then turned to her with a devilish look on his face. "You painted me in the buff?"

She answered with a playful look of her own. "Yes. And you're buying the painting without even seeing it?" She giggled as he tickled her neck with his tongue. "Not a wise investment."

"Huh. I think it's a damn good investment." He licked along her collarbone. "I can't believe you sent it to the art dealer."

She threaded her fingers in his hair. "You're the one who wanted to show my work, remember?"

He slipped his hands beneath her and cupped her bottom in his hands. "Your landscapes."

"This one has a landscape."

"And me naked in it?"

"Well, that, too." She traced a finger down to his navel, stirring his sex. "But the real thing is better."

He braced himself above her and slid over her skin, the whisper of his breath so erotic she bucked beneath him. "Really?"

"Yes, really." She moaned as he claimed her.

"You found out I took your painting and you wanted revenge, didn't you?"

She dug her fingers into the corded muscles of his arms. "I guess I did."

He stroked her breast with his tongue, tormenting the hardened pebble tip. "I like a woman with spunk. But I might have to get some revenge of my own."

"Oh." Rebecca snuggled down beneath him and let him have his way.

His revenge was the sweetest thing she could ever have imagined.

Epilogue

"You may kiss the bride."

Thomas lifted the bridal veil and pulled Rebecca into his arms, then pressed his lips to hers to seal the vows they had just professed. Rebecca closed her eyes and savored the moment. This was the happiest day of her life.

Alison had helped plan their wedding in a matter of weeks, Mimi had catered the reception, her father had given her away with tears in his eyes, and her sister, Suzanne, and her cousins had all been bridesmaids. And Grammy Rose had taken the bride's book from her hope chest. Now it was filled with names of all their friends from Sugar Hill.

The kiss slowly ended, and Thomas offered his arm. They raced down the aisle to the squeals and cheers of all their family and friends, then were bombarded with congratulations. The reception passed in a blur of hugs and kisses and cake and laughter. They even danced on the lawn in front of the gazebo with the beautiful mountain scenery as a backdrop.

"How are Dad and Uncle Wiley holding up?" Rebecca whispered to Suzanne later when she finally had time to breathe.

"Keeping to separate sides of the lawn," Suzanne said. "For now."

Rebecca laughed. Sure enough, Mimi and Maggie Rose had Wiley cornered, while Hannah and Jake tracked her father. She wondered if the two men would ever end their brotherly feud. And if her father's wife would be able to fill the void her mother had left. She wanted to see him happy again. This time she thought she detected a spark of true affection between them.

She turned to Suzanne, grateful she and her sister had gotten closer. "Thanks for being my maid of honor, Suzanne."

"I wouldn't have wanted it any other way. You are the most beautiful bride, sis." Suzanne hugged her, and they both wiped at the tears. "Guess what? It looks like I'm going to be spending a good bit of time in Sugar Hill in the future."

"You're moving to Sugar Hill?" Rebecca asked.

"Heavens, no," Suzanne said. "But my boss is looking for some property nearby to develop. He thinks there is a run-down ranch around that we could snap up for next to nothing. From some down-on-his-luck cowboy who's fallen on hard times."

"You mean Rafe McAllister?"

"I think that was his name."

"Gertrude said he's the guy who won Uncle Wiley's purple pickup truck."

"Really?"

"Yes." Rebecca frowned. "But I doubt he'll sell,

Suzanne. I think that property's been in his family for ages.''

''He may not have a choice,'' Suzanne said.

''Just be careful, I've heard he's pretty tough.''

Suzanne winked. ''Nothing I can't handle, sis. He won't know what hit him when I get ahold of him.''

Rebecca laughed at her sister's cockiness, but she still wasn't sure. Rafe McAllister was supposedly tough, macho, and had once been a troublemaker in the town when he was younger.

What would happen when he met her sister? Especially when Suzanne tried to buy his ranch out from under him?

''Time to throw the bouquet!'' Grammy Rose shouted.

Rebecca laughed, remembering a few short weeks ago when she'd caught Alison's. Her cousins, Caitlin and Angie, and Suzanne all crowded together, along with Gertrude and Grammy Rose and a few of her grandmother's friends. They laughed and argued back and forth over who should catch the bouquet. Rebecca turned her back to the group and tossed the lilies over her shoulder, then spun around when squeals rang out.

Her sister, Suzanne, stood holding the flowers, her odd look almost comical. Caitlin and Angie moaned that they should have caught it, but Grammy Rose looked at Rebecca and winked.

Rebecca smiled back, her heart so full of love and joy she was almost bursting.

Did Grammy Rose already have Suzanne's hope chest waiting? And what kind of surprises had she put inside for her sister?

* * * * *

Check out what's inside Suzanne's hope chest
in
HAVE COWBOY, NEED CUPID
Coming next month from
Harlequin American Romance